THE SHIP OF WIDOWS

I. GREKOVA

Translated and with an Introduction by
CATHY PORTER

Published by VIRAGO PRESS Limited 1985
41 William IV Street, London WC2N 4DB

First published in the USSR 1981 by *Novy Mir*

British Library Cataloguing in Publication Data

Grekova, I.
The ship of widows.
I. Title
891.73'44 [F] PG3476.G6
ISBN 0-86068-487-3
ISBN 0-86068-492-X Pbk

Printed in Great Britain by litho at
Anchor Brendon Ltd, Tiptree, Essex

I. Grekova is one of the Soviet Union's most popular short-story writers. A mathematician, author of a famous textbook on the theory of probability, one of the few women in the Soviet Union to be awarded the degree of Doctor of Sciences, Elena Sergeevna Ventzel began writing fiction in her mid-fifties, taking as her pseudonym I. Grekova, meaning the mathematical symbol for an unknown quantity. In 1962 her first published story, 'Behind the Gate', appeared in *Novy Mir (New World)*, the Soviet Union's leading literary-political magazine. I. Grekova worked at the Zhukovsky Military Academy until 1967, when her unheroic story 'On Manoeuvres' was thought to be incompatible with her job there, and she took a less prestigious job at a non-military institute. Her next published story did not appear until 1979, followed by 'The Ship of Widows' in 1981. Never before published in English it has been translated and introduced by Cathy Porter, author of *Alexandra Kollontai: a biography*.

I. Grekova has three children and lives in Moscow.

INTRODUCTION

'The Ship of Widows' appeared in the literary-political magazine *Novy Mir* (*New World*) in May 1981. *Novy Mir* is by far the most popular such magazine in the Soviet Union, and its influence there extends far beyond its comparatively small circulation – about 150,000 in a country where readers are measured in millions and literary debates conducted with a passion quite foreign to us here. In the west *Novy Mir* is known for its publication of controversial writers and for little else.

It was in 1957, a year after the liberalising twentieth Party Congress, that *Novy Mir's* then editor Konstantin Simonov serialised Vladimir Dudintsev's novel *Not By Bread Alone*. Thousands of meetings were held and articles written to discuss the work, until Khrushchev stepped in to describe it as slanderous, and to urge Dudintsev to pursue more positive themes. Many conservatives in the government were outraged by the novel's graphic depiction of Stalinist repression. But by then many others were standing up to describe their experiences of the Stalin years, and *Novy Mir*, under its new editor, Alexander Tvardovsky, played a prominent part in promoting this process. Yet most of *Novy Mir's* writers are still unknown outside Russia.

In 1962 Tvardovsky published 'Za prokhodnoi' ('Behind the Gate'*), the first published story of I. Grekova. This is a pseudonym, meaning the mathematical symbol for an unknown quantity. The author's real name is Elena Sergeevna Ventzel; she is a mathematician, one of a very small number of women to be awarded the degree of Doctor of Sciences, author of a widely used textbook on the theory of probability, and until 1967 a professor at the Zhukovsky Military Academy. Apart from this, tantalisingly little seems to be know about her. At all events, her pseudonym indicates her desire to keep her writing seperate from the other parts of her life, and she has always resisted Tvardovsky's encouragement to write full time. ('What me? A

* Her soviet publishers translate this as 'Outside a Gatekeeper's Office', and an emigré critic translates it as 'On the Inside'. The first, I felt, was too prosaic, the second too sinister.

respectable mother of three children? I might as well go on the streets!') What she has published over the past twenty years, however, has established her as one of the Soviet Union's most popular short-story writers.

Several stories have appeared in the papers *Literary Russia* ('Rothschild's Violin' in 1981, 'Famous People' in 1982), and *Soviet Russia* (a fairystory called 'The Striped Stone' in 1979). There are also a number of articles, including two for the *Literary Gazette*, newspaper of the Writers' Union: 'Ten Roles of Women in the Contemporary Family' in 1981, and 'The Law of the Living Word: The Development of Modern Literary and Spoken Russian' in 1982. And she has been interviewed – in 1981 by the paper *Soviet Industry* ('Preparing Specialists, Not Robinson Crusoes'), and in 1983 by *Literary Gazette* ('Without Wasting Words'). But her best works have appeared in *Novy Mir*, and it is with *Novy Mir* that her career as a writer is identified.

'Behind the Gate' is about a team of young scientists working in a secret laboratory. As they campaign to work a ten-hour rather than an eight-hour day, and argue for and against the need for lyrical poetry (one of them is a lyrical poet and reads out some of his own poems), it emerges that they are working on a project to make the Black Box, and that their heroic labour is going to destroy the world.

Her second story, 'Ladies' Hairdresser', is about a young man, Vitalii, who is prevented from creating the fantastic hairstyles he wants to and goes off to become a carpenter instead. In 'Hotel Manageress', I. Grekova describes the loving and obedient wife of a despotic army officer who discovers new talents and resources in herself after his death. Her next story, 'On Manoeuvres', about a group of soldiers living in a dull garrison town, appeared in July 1967, and paints a devastatingly unfavourable picture of life in the Red Army.

Over the past few years *Novy Mir* had been receiving more and more stories, essays and novels about Stalin's prisons, and more and more of its writers were touching on themes of punishment and repression. In 1966 the magazine was severely criticised for its over-fondness for this kind of literature; Grekova's unheroic view of the army in 'On Manoeuvres' was felt to be incompatible with her job at the Zhukovsky Academy, and at the end of 1967 she moved to another job at a non-military institute. No more of her stories were published until 'The Striped Stone' in 1979. And then in May 1981 'The Ship of Widows' appeared in *Novy Mir*.

'My husband was killed at the front, right at the beginning of the war': Olga Ivanovna's opening words set the tone for this story of five women's lives during the war and peace of the last forty years. Their lives are those of many Russian women: after the war they outnumbered men eight to one. This group of Moscow widows are forced by the war to live together in a communal flat and, despite the incalculable sufferings and sacrifices of the war, they are able to create a new, and in many ways very liberating kind of family life for themselves.

But then there are memories of an earlier war to sustain them. For many women the civil war which followed the Bolshevik revolution of 1917 was a time of immense excitement and hope. Thousands joined the Red Army, as nurses, spies, guerrillas and public speakers. The old repressive family (of which Kapa in the story was a victim) was dead and buried, and the Bolsheviks pledged themselves to put something better in its place. The marriage law of 1917 simplified marriage and divorce, a law of 1920 legalised abortion, and the new Family Code of 1926 removed restrictions on divorce and recognised *de facto* marriages.

But despite all this humane legislation, the transformation of family life was a deeply painful process, especially for women, and the five in the story are still experiencing its effects. Women in the civil war whose husbands had died or left them had a desperately hard struggle to support themselves and their children. Those who followed them, like Anfisa in the story, continued to have their health, energy and confidence sapped by the daily anguish of their double burden, and by dirty, crowded living conditions. Many women, however, like Panka in the story, loved the freedom of working for the Bolsheviks in the early heady days of the revolution, and saw the experiences of both the civil war and the Second World War – with their spartan creches, ramshackle canteens and crowded communal flats – as a model for things to come. The cultured Olga Ivanovna doesn't share working-class Panka's aspirations, however, and it is differences like these that Grekova explores in describing the tensions and friendships between the five women. But it is the growing friendship between Olga Ivanovna and the uneducated Anfisa Maximovna on which the story concentrates. And indeed so closely do the two women identify with one another that at times the narrative focus leaps, sometimes quite disconcertingly, from Olga Ivanovna to Anfisa Maximovna and back again.

The five women are brought together by their shared experiences of war. But in general these experiences are veiled. Olga Ivanovna loses her daughter, husband, mother – everything. Anfisa Maximovna's husband is called up immediately. Every Russian had their tragedy in these four desperate years of war. But despite indescribable living conditions, the trauma of constant bombing and the ceaseless death toll of friends and relatives, people worked as never before. Hitler's war of extermination against the Russian people had a devastating effect on the morale of his soldiers and increased the Russians' resistance: it was a genuine people's war, and memories of it are still painfully alive in the Soviet Union today. Soviet art, literature and film continue to celebrate these experiences, and I. Grekova describes the five widows' struggling lives in a style that is all the more moving for being so spare and laconic.

Most soviet novels and films present the Nazi invasion in the summer of 1941 as a complete surprise, and indeed many Muscovites were setting off on their summer holidays when it came. 'It was apparently impossible to prepare oneself in advance for such a tragedy,' wrote Simonov in his famous novel *The Living And The Dead*. Within three weeks German troops had seized white Russia and the Ukraine. The Red Army was routed, the Red Airforce incapacitated, the Russian position was thought to be hopeless. And German troops ploughed on towards Moscow, Hitler's main target.

For these first three weeks people in Moscow remained in good spirits – or rather they sleepwalked. The streets were crowded with smartly dressed people, the shops were full, there were no food shortages, no coupons in any case. Fourteen theatres were open – and invariably packed – and theatres and restaurants continued to do good business. Few talked openly of war. But people were preparing for it nonetheless. Men were forming themselves into home defence teams, more and more soldiers were to be seen marching up and down the streets (usually singing), a midnight curfew was imposed. And as Olga Ivanovna recalls in the story, there was a mania for spies – militia men and women would pounce on people and order them to put out cigarettes and torches, for fear they might be signalling to enemy aircraft.

More and more posters appeared on the walls: one of a Russian tank crushing a giant crab with a Hitler moustache; another of a Red soldier ramming a bayonet down the throat of a Hitler-faced rat. There were exhortations: 'Women go and work on the collective farms! Replace the men now in the army!' Many houses would paste up the morning's edition of *Pravda* or *Izvestia*, and people would crowd round to read.

More and more men were called up. Anfisa Maximovna's husband Fyodor goes off telling her to wait for him; and in those terrible months 'Wait for me' and Simonov's poem of that name, written to his wife from the front, became a sort of prayer for millions of Russian women like Anfisa.

Anfisa's first move is to get back her old factory job. Practically all the work in the war industries, down the mines and on the farms was now done by women, under unspeakable conditions. Many women worked as many as fourteen hours a day in the factories, with almost no food and no holidays. Several million men and women were evacuated to Siberia and the Urals, where they worked often to the point of exhaustion and death, to reconstruct key industries. On the farms women stood in not only for men, but for horses and tractors too.

But many women preferred to be at the front line, and joined the Red Army as machine gunners, nurses, pilots and navigators.

Anfisa trains as a nurse and leaves for the front to look for Fyodor. There she nurses men who have braved hell and returned damaged and dependent – as are all the men in her life. There is Grisha the horse thief, who seduces her and makes her pregnant, Fyodor, who returns crippled and broken after being given up for dead, and especially her son Vadim, an angry, tyrannical little patriarch, for whom she gladly sacrifices her health, sleep and freedom, and for whom she eventually destroys herself.

Many hundred women and children were evacuated from Moscow in the early days of the war, and for the first week the stations were crowded with women weeping for fear they might not return. (Olga Ivanovna misses the evacuation in the chaos and stays behind with her dazed mother and daughter.) By the second week in July food was running short and Moscow was preparing for air raids. Firewatching was organised on a vast scale, the city was encircled by three rings of anti-aircraft defences, and dozens of searchlights lit the sky when the first raid came, on the night of 21 July. Next morning there were a few broken windows, a few fires and a few bomb craters (one in Red Square), but only fifteen German planes out of a hundred had got through, and the only people injured were firewatchers. But as raid followed raid the atmosphere became grimmer, the losses heavier, the jokes fewer. People began to lose dangerous amounts of sleep, ambulances were in short supply, there were only local first-aid teams to deal with the wounded and dying. Yet people continued to pack the

Moscow Arts Theatre for its latest productions (*The School for Scandal* and *Anna Karenina*). On 30 September, just a few days before Hitler's 'final offensive' on Moscow, the Bolshoi was putting on *Swan Lake*.

Hitler's 'final offensive' speech was omitted from the soviet press and it took people several days to realise how serious this offensive was. By the second week in October people in Moscow were being called on to build defence lines inside and outside the city, and when the Germans reached the outskirts of Moscow they were met by detachments of workers fighting, at devastating cost of life, with home-made implements and petrol bombs.

That autumn and winter Moscow struggled for its life. Only half its population was still in the city. Those that were there were cold and hungry. The chemists had run out of medicine and anaesthetics. The streets were filled with soldiers on their way to or back from the front. Russian fighter planes patrolled the skies, Russian and German guns could be heard booming in the distance. There was a rapid succession of air raids. The Bolshoi was bombed, yet half a dozen theatres continued to perform plays, concerts and ballets. And people who had lost everything refused to break. 'There wasn't enough of anything, but there was always music,' says Olga Ivanovna, as she too struggles back to life. 'Flow on, little trickle of culture, and help people to live.'

In Leningrad nearly three million people were trapped by the Germans for almost three years and condemned to starve. In the summer of 1942 thousands were dying in the battle of Stalingrad. In Moscow that summer the atmosphere was extraordinarily charged. One observer recalls the 'countless tears produced on one of the worst days of July by the famous love theme in Tchaikovsky's *Romeo and Juliet*. The first performance of Shostakovich's *Seventh Symphony* in this period had a stunning impact. Writers like Ehrenburg, Simonov, Surkov and Akhmatova expressed both the warmth and tenderness people felt for Russia in her hour of danger, and their hatred for the Germans.

By the beginning of 1943 people were slowly beginning to hope again. Despite devastating losses, Russia had built up an effective and powerfully equipped army, while Germany's was in fast decline. In February the Germans capitulated at Stalingrad. That summer victory salvoes rang out in Moscow for the recapture of Kursk, and now Moscow itself was out of danger. By the end of that year most of the territory overrun by the Germans had been liberated, and the Leningrad blockade had been broken. Life was still grim: beautiful

Leningrad, with its museums and palaces and proud revolutionary traditions had been mutilated by shells, and a million of its citizens had starved to death. Men were still being drafted, and women and old people were still working desperately long hours in the factories. Everyone had lost someone, and suffered in various terrible ways. Russia had lost twenty million of her people, a further twenty million had been injured or disabled, twenty million were homeless, 11,710 towns and 70,000 villages had been destroyed. There were many Russians – like Anfisa's returning husband Fyodor – who could not believe that Hitler was dead long after he and Goebbels had killed themselves.

Children like Anfisa's son Vadim who were born at the end of the war would suffer its effects all their lives. Some four million children's fathers were killed or missing, their mothers out all day toiling in the factories. Classrooms were horribly overcrowded and teachers overworked. There was a marked increase in juvenile delinquency and thieving.

Vadim too suffers. Filled with anger and the desire for revenge, forgiving nothing and trusting no one, he gradually becomes the focus for each of the five widows' unrealised hopes and longings, and eventually takes over the story. Yet the story's conclusion is a hopeful one, with its emphasis on Russia's reconstruction and recovery. Russia's war losses, beyond anything we could imagine, joined with a sense of pride and purpose as people began to rebuild their devastated land. Vadim's wounds too start slowly to heal. Desperate to escape the smothering presence of the widows, he goes off to work in the remote virgin lands. And there, in an almost Tolstoyan episode of redemption, he conquers boredom and hardship and rediscovers his love for his mother.

In Moscow, life slowly returned to normal. People started to relax. One or two commercial restaurants opened up, a few expensive luxuries appeared in the shops. Women like Anfisa, who had spent the war working and bringing up children on their own, now longed only for a little security and comfort.

Women had fought in the civil war. They had been mobilised in vast numbers from 1928 to 1937 to fulfil the First and Second Five-Year Plans. They had played a heroic part in the defeat of Hitler. Yet despite the extraordinary transformation of their lives and the fragmentation of traditional family life, the old family patterns struggled now to reassert themselves. And as men returned from the war to take back the jobs occupied by their wives and rebuild their shattered families, women were expected to surrender their old independence.

The Family Code of 1944 was an expression of people's longing for a more stable family life, but its particularly cruel and draconian form highlighted many of the strains and tensions in family relations in war-torn Russia – and indeed in the whole period since the revolution. Divorce was made harder. There was a heavy tax on bachelors over twenty-five and on couples with less than three children; there were various medals and financial grants for mothers of five children or more. Children born out of wedlock would have a blank space on their birth certificates, and men were to be protected from paternity suits.

There were many women, however, who deeply resented having to give up their hard-won independence, and the law had many bitter critics, although it was only after Stalin's death in 1953 that these criticisms were voiced and the law was finally reformed.

In 'The Ship of Widows' it is a very different kind of family life that the five women are struggling to make together, and Grekova does not minimise their difficulties in adjusting to it. Their friendships, made and broken in the clash of cultures and classes, are often painful. But these friendships ennoble common feelings and communal passions, so that at the end, at Anfisa Maximovna's funeral, Olga Ivanovna finally learns to weep, and in weeping for her friend is able to weep for all she has lost.

Cathy Porter, London, 1984

[1]

My husband was killed at the front right at the beginning of the war. We stayed on in Moscow, 'we' being my old mother, by then more dead than alive, my fourteen-year-old daughter Natasha, and me. I was in a sort of torpor, and simply couldn't act. We didn't manage to be evacuated in time, and later in all the chaos it was too late. I was, however, offered a place in a car going east, leaving from the courtyard of some obscure institution. People rushed over there, documents from a dispersed archive flew through the air. One place? Naturally I refused. Then I wavered: 'Should I send Natasha?' And then, 'No, I can't let her go.' The car left. I told them about it when I got home, still doubting the correctness of my decision. 'You did right,' said Mother. 'If we perish, we'll all perish together.' She was always trying to keep her spirits up; she was dry and neat and did a lot of knitting, clicking her needles in one's ear and muttering as she counted the stitches. Natasha understood absolutely nothing, and used to sing in the mornings as she tied her ribbons in front of the mirror. It horrified me how easily she had survived her father's death. I now realise that this was because life was simply unreal to her, but at the time I often longed to hit her.

So in the end we stayed where we were – it was easier to do nothing. We lived as we had done in the old days in our old house, in an old flat with high curved windows overlooking a courtyard where multicoloured underwear hung peacefully to dry and provincial charm wreathed the balconies in ivy. I had no work. I sold a few things at the flea-market and bought or bartered some things to eat. Autumn strode in, frost nipped the fingers in the mornings, the ivy turned crimson, then withered. Life developed a pattern, order was re-established in the town after the chaotic days of the hurried evacuation. They gave out ration cards, organised a blackout, and little boys searched for spies, who flashed signals to the enemy from their attics; I once saw one of these signals, a bright, eerie flash. The most extraordinarily outlandish things, like crabs and champagne appeared in the shops at times. People would form long queues for them, laughing: 'What are we queuing for?' I once stood in one of these queues, and afterwards we ate crab and drank champagne all night and Natasha strummed her guitar. There was something profoundly profane about these nocturnal festivities. German planes flew overhead from time to time, but they didn't frighten me; nothing frightened me, so convinced was I that the worst had already happened, and that nothing bad could possibly happen to our family now. Anyway the raids were comparatively rare and their effects went almost unnoticed on the huge face of the city. The debris would be cleared quickly, and a public garden hurriedly knocked up in its place. Barrage balloons ruled the city – giant sausages steered during the day by girls in military uniforms, and in the evening hoisted by guards into the soft clear sky. There was something so hopeful about their calm, corpulent presence: go to sleep people, they said. The familiar voice from the loudspeaker blaring out the familiar words: 'Citizens, air-raid warning!' no longer frightened us either, and when we heard it we would unhurriedly put on our clothes. The bomb-shelter was not in our house but in a neighbouring house across the courtyard, and I always felt as though we were taking up someone else's space there. Besides, Mother was quite helpless, and it was sheer torture trying to drag her over there. And how could one endlessly go on explaining it to her? So in the the end we simply stopped going.

Late one evening after the all-clear there was another warning. Natasha raised her head irritably from the pillow and said: 'Not another warning, Mother? I'm fed up with them!' And I replied: 'It doesn't matter darling, go back to sleep.' Those were the last words we said to one another, because later that night our house was destroyed by a bomb. Mother and Natasha perished – I didn't. I was saved by a miracle, as they say. A miracle? Rather one of those negative miracles, miracles of evil, wrought by the devil himself. My spine, a leg and both arms were fractured. Strange as it may seem, I was conscious throughout. I remember the weight of a brick pressing down on me, and a door hanging terrifyingly askew above my head. I remember thinking: 'Mother? Natasha?' and then thinking: 'This is the end.' When they dragged me out I shrieked 'Careful!' as I was trying to protect my arms.

Then there was an interlude of complete unconsciousness. The first sensation I was conscious of was a crushing weight – a weight, not a pain. I imagined this was the brick, which they hadn't removed for some reason. Only much later did I realise that it wasn't a brick at all, it was plaster. It surrounded me on all sides, I was enclosed by it, immured in it. Besides the weight I felt nothing. I was blind. I was surrounded in darkness, not an indistinct grey but a fiery black, which could mean only one thing – I was blind. Sparks flashed in the darkness occasionally, star-shaped flashes of light. They jumped around, always in the same direction. Once I opened my mouth and said: 'Mother? Natasha?' but I could hear nothing. I was deaf.

So in this deaf darkness passed a timeless time marked only by the flash of jumping sparks; they appeared at regular intervals which I couldn't measure, knowing only that they were regular and that they formed a clear and patterned rhythm. The sparks themselves were very beautiful, somewhat reminiscent of living beings, but their inexorable movement from one side to another wasn't from the living world.

My sight returned to me before my hearing. After an indefinitely long time I began to see the light. It glimmered and wavered in a watery-grey room which resembled an aquarium, with a large white fish hanging in the air-water above my face. I opened my mouth to say the same thing: 'Mama? Natasha?' and once again I could hear nothing. The white fish flipped its tail and sped past at great speed. Then it turned out that it wasn't a fish at all but the white headscarf of a nurse. And beneath the headscarf, on a yellow, rather puffy face, two great eyes were shining with earnest astonishment. 'So I'm in hospital and I'm not blind,' I thought, and looked down my body towards my legs. On my bed lay something white and very big which, judging by the place it occupied, must have been me, but it wasn't – it felt like a dull, alien weight. They poured something warm and tasteless into my mouth.

I regained consciousness gradually, but at an uneven rate, in jumps. Sound came back shortly after light, also in sparks and flashes, at first quite painful. Once I opened my eyes and saw my friend sitting beside me in tears. The sound of her weeping was loud and reminded me of hiccoughs. 'Mother? Natasha?' I said, and heard my own voice, like a harsh shriek. My friend did not reply but I knew from her face that they were dead. I was encased in plaster from head to foot, and could neither struggle nor move my arms, nor kill myself. They poured something warm into my mouth again. Unconsciousness, blackness returned. I think I entreated it to be eternal. I would regain consciousness for a while, and it would flicker and vanish again. The emotional pain was not constant, it would burst out unexpectedly, and then it was unendurable – then it seemed it would shatter the plaster from within.

I spent another year after that in hospital while the

doctors battled for my life, for which I had absolutely no use. During that year my longing for death, at first so strong, gradually subsided and was replaced by a hatred of the plaster and a longing not to kill myself now but the plaster. Then there began to appear glimmerings of interest, now blazing up, now sinking away, in the world outside the window. It was accessible only to my peripheral vision at first, but nevertheless it felt like something big and beautiful. Later on when my neck vertebrae were released, I turned my head and the outside world was fully revealed, and it was indeed beautiful. The branches were stirring, the rain was falling, the pigeons were strutting, and it was all so fresh and bright, so much brighter than in ordinary life. I had never seen such blue pigeons before. From the distance of time that brightness has dimmed slightly, but I have kept something of it to this day, so that I am occasionally struck, say, by the brightness of the rain.

So I could already turn my head. Now I wanted to get better, if possible – and it turned out that it was. One beautiful sun-filled day they replaced the thick solid plaster with a lighter kind, ecstatically light, almost weightless. And on that day I fraternised with the flies flying weightlessly around the sunny ward. A little later I was able to sit on my bed, move my arms and eat. It would be impossible for someone who hasn't gone hungry to imagine the place the meagre food in those days had in people's lives. The receiving of meals was virtually transformed into a ceremony. I was amazed to find myself waiting with such trepidation for dinner to be handed out, but trepidation it undoubtedly was. Shuffling footsteps would be heard, dishes would clatter, the nurse would appear in her down-at-heel slippers, exposing her bare amber-coloured heels, and dinner would be served. I would eat, then sleep – long and deep, like an infant.

When I was discharged it turned out that I had partly lost the use of my hands, so that meant the end of yet something else – for I was a pianist by profession. But this loss meant little to me beside all the others. I had never really been very good. My talent had conferred on me nothing but a savage dissatisfaction with myself and an implacable conscience, which forced me to practise endlessly – by day on the grand piano and by night ineffectually drumming my fingers on my knee – and that isn't enough. So they gave me a third-class invalidity benefit and sent me out into the world. I remember encountering that world when I walked out of the hospital gates, how I stood there, mindlessly gulping air, dazed by the sunlight, while my friend held my elbow.

I stayed with her for the first few weeks. But this arrangement couldn't continue indefinitely, and I began to look for my own living space. 'But what do you need it for?' said my friend. 'Why don't you stay here with me?' But I simply couldn't have done that – I am ashamed to say she irritated me. She was in an ecstasy of self-sacrifice, she was talkative, quarrelsome and cried a lot, and she seemed to expect the same from me. But I couldn't cry – the things inside me would not turn into tears . . . And her despotic concern for me! It nearly drove me mad! She would shout at me in a genuine rage, for instance, if I went out without a scarf. As if a mere scarf mattered, as if I mattered, as if any of us mattered, when we were all so useless in the face of mighty world events . . . She never listened to the radio, or read the papers, and she was constantly immersed in petty anxieties. Whenever we ate dinner together she would always divide up the food painstakingly into two unequal shares, and always try to push the bigger share towards me, at which I would protest, and a ridiculous exchange of plates would ensue . . . No, I needed my own corner, my own four walls.

The regional soviet quite quickly allocated me a room whose previous occupants had either died or moved out. It turned out to be quite small, made even smaller by its elegant oblong shape, with a high smoke-blackened ceiling. The window overlooked a courtyard at the back filled with rows of blue rubbish bins, and a bright orange cat prowled around in the background, shielding itself with its tail, like a flag. It all seemed quite beautiful to me, especially the setting sunlight on the cat's fiery coat. The previous occupants had left a bed, evidently abandoned because it was useless; the webbing had worn thin and here and there had been roughly tied up with bits of string. I sat down on it and the webbing gave way and creaked. The iron under my knees was exquisitely cool. Yes, I loved it all, I would have liked to keep this emptiness, this simplicity, this brightness. I didn't want to acquire a lot of things. They say that ships encrusted with barnacles lose speed, and I didn't want to lose speed; even though I had nowhere to go, I dreamed of the joys of lightness, and my dislike of possessions has remained with me to this day.

My friend gave me some essentials – a table, a chair, a mattress and a blanket, some plates and underclothes. She wanted to give me more things, to shower me with gifts, but I wouldn't take them. I remember a stupid argument we had about some very solid item she called a 'causette', which I wanted in my room as much as I wanted a mangy dog. My friend insisted, I firmly said 'I'd rather die' – she cried. I didn't. Now I wish I'd taken it.

* *

We soon had to part company. My friend had to visit her married daughter in Siberia. She was terrified at the prospect of leaving and could not speak of it without weeping. But I was so hard-hearted. I should have understood her anxiety, her exhaustion, her premonitions . . . The tears poured down her emaciated cheeks as she put on her glasses to make a note of her address for me, and seeing her aged face I realised that neither of us was young any longer. When we said goodbye she shoved a wad of money into my hands and said: 'Give it back when you can afford to.' But I never did give that money back, for shortly afterwards she died. I don't know where her grave is or if there are flowers on it, and if so which flowers. I tried to post the money to her daughter, but the postal order was returned with the words 'Addressee gone away'. I am tormented to this day by that unreturned debt, along with my other countless debts and sins.

When my friend left I was completely alone. No relatives (they'd all died), no workmates (they'd all gone away), not even any of my old neighbours (the building had been destroyed and they'd put up a little park in its place). In the past I had always been sustained by my worries about other people, and other people's worries about me. The word 'unworried' is generally associated with the notion of happiness. But how forlorn and vulnerable a life without worries is! It took me a long time to adapt to it. At first I couldn't even cook for myself; it seemed barbaric to eat.

* *

The money my friend left me eventually came to an end and I had to get a job. There was no point in thinking of my former profession of course – I resigned myself uncomplainingly to this, and was secretly relieved that I should no longer have to agonise over my lack of talent . . . It was all one to me where I worked, but what could I do? What skill did I have? I was no good for any sort of physical labour, and as for intellectual work . . . probably not that either.

'What sort of education have you had?' they asked me.

'Conservatoire,' I said, embarrassed. 'Piano class.'

'Can you play?'

'No.'

'So what are we going to do with you, comrade? We'll have a think about it, you come back later.'

They thought, I came back – again and again and again, but there was no work. I felt like a supplicant begging for alms. After the rejection (for rejection it invariably was, although invariably delayed), my shaking hands would gather up my things – a little shopping bag containing bread or potatoes, a gnarled walking-stick and another bag containing my certificates, which took the place of my documents. Sometimes these certificates would fall on the floor and I would pick them up, mortified by my crippled condition and their pity for me, which they expressed by fidgeting in their seats and twitching their hands. Then I would wrap myself up in my shawl and leave the room without looking back, fearing that they would offer me money on account of my beggarly appearance.

Several months passed in this way and I had already started to lose hope when I was suddenly offered a job! Yes, a real job as a music teacher in the House of the Child.

'What is the House of the Child?' I asked.

'It's rather like a children's home, but it's only for the youngest, from birth to three years. Commonly described as a creche.' It was my employer who described it thus, the inspector of arts education. He was a huge man with a terrifying temper and red hair in his nostrils. He had work piled up above his head and a desk littered with documents and papers. He tapped his pencil rhythmically as he spoke to me.

'Well then, everything clear?'

I hesitated. The offer terrified me and stirred up the depths of my own lack of confidence. I didn't know anything, couldn't do anything. But it was a job, and I had to work in order to live. And I had to live – for some unknown reason I absolutely had to live! Never before had I been so hungry for life. I was thrilled and fascinated by the world in all its aspects: the mauve asphalt of the streets, the smoke drifting into the sky, the green of last year's grass poking through the dirty snow like a crude symbol of immortality. And living things too – cats, pigeons, children with their business and secrets!

It wasn't that I'd forgotten my grief. No, that grief lived on inside me, that grief was sacred, yet life was so infinitely fascinating.

The pencil tapped peremptorily.

'I'm waiting for your answer, Comrade Flerova. Does the job suit you?'

The tapping meant don't delay. Even this terrifying man interested me.

'It suits me but . . . I'm afraid I may not be able to cope.'

'Rubbish! "Siskin Snowman, where have you been?"' He sang in a high falsetto. 'Well, can you play Siskin?'

I looked at my hands and stretched my fingers. 'Yes I can.'

'Well that's all right then. We'll tell you how to get to the House of the Child. And don't be bashful! Cheer up old mother, it's not so bad!'

I think this was the first time anyone had called me 'old mother', and I wasn't quite forty at the time. Later on I was called everything – old lady, grandma, even 'Baba Yaga'. I walked with a stick, my back was bent, and little boys would run after me shouting: 'Baba Yaga! Wooden Leg!'*

You get used to anything.

[2]

The House of the Child where they'd assigned me a job was situated in the outskirts of the city, in one of those side streets where Moscow stops being Moscow and the remote provinces crawl out of its face. Ancient hollow

*Baba Yaga is a bad witch in Russian folk stories.

trees spread out their branches and beneath them huddled rickety little cottages, a blotched mauvish-grey colour, like rain-washed, weather-beaten planks of wood. As a tribute to the times, cross-shaped paper stickers were still up in the windows – a naive method of saving the glass during air-raids: people were very keen on them at the beginning of the war. But now it was the beginning of spring, a weak, sunny beginning, smelling of earth, damp branches and the future. I walked down the side street leaning on my crutch and marvelling at the free and supple movements of a woman carrying her buckets from the street water-fountain. How smoothly the yoke swayed on her shoulder as she walked, scattering full-bodied sparkling drops of water in her wake. On the trees some birds, probably crows, clamoured gutturally in a cabal. The dilapidated, spring-like charm of the little cottages, the paper crosses and the crows' nests touched me with hope and the promise of life. There was a loudspeaker on the corner broadcasting cheerful news about the situation at the front. Beneath it stood an old man in frayed felt boots; he had thrown his head back and the sun was shining through his beard.

The House of the Child, at the end of the street behind a high fence, was also alert in anticipation of new life. In the garden between the melting, dirt-speckled snowdrifts groups of very young, quiet children walked in pairs along the paths under the supervision of a teacher. They were modestly and poorly dressed in identical little state-issue quilted jackets. It was a two-storey stone building, encircled by verandahs and smothered in ivy, bare and withered by the winter, yet yearning to live. As I approached the house I was struck by a quiet chorus of little wailing voices drifting through the open ventilation window of one of the wings. A woman in a white overall came out of the house with a wooden bucket in her hand.

'What's that?' I asked her, meaning the quiet chorus.

'The breast-feeders crying,' she replied. 'Well that's

what we call them anyway, even though there aren't any breasts to feed them. They have no mothers – some died, some've abandoned them. Ours are all artificially fed. They're plagued with rickets, but never mind, we soldier on. So what can I do for your, my dear?'

She had a gentle, full face, with yellowish eyes and thick lips slighly covered in light down.

'I want to talk to the directress,' I said. 'I've been sent to work here.'

The woman laughed and waved her bucket towards the house. Yet another one, she seemed to be saying; they keep sending these people to work here. No they definitely won't take me, I decided. What use am I to them with my 'Siskin Snowman'?

In the passageway stood a battery of bottles filled with greyish milk, neatly stoppered with wads of cotton wool. The door into the directress's office was open. I went in. An elderly woman with lines of anxiety on her yellow face was counting on an abacus. I put my permit on the table.

'Just a moment,' she said, continuing her calculations, 'I haven't got ten hands. The bookkeeper is sick. And what about my health?'

Standing up was hard for me, so I sat down. Click, click, click went the abacus. The sun shone in through the window. A delicate piercing shadow from the ivy moved cautiously across the table and over the directress's yellow hands. The chorus of infants was not so audible from here; it sang out faintly, a weak musical lament, a note of grief. 'No, they won't take me,' I thought again. 'It's too good here.'

The directress finished counting, moved aside her abacus and took my application form. 'How's your arithmetic?'

'Not very good,' I answered, hurriedly trying to remember my multiplication table.

'Me too. Twice two I know, no higher. I desperately

need people for the paper work. We want working hands, and who do they send? One foot in the grave.'

I stood up to leave, clutching my shopping bag and handbag.

'Wait a bit, don't rush!' she shouted. 'I didn't mean to be nasty, it's just a cry from the heart. I have to share it with someone! If you don't talk about it and keep it all to yourself you burst!'

I said nothing.

'You have to see it from my position. There are no nannies here. Nyurka's taken it into her head to go to the factory, can't sit still, corkscrew up her backside. There are no fitters, the buckets are all worn out, we can't get any milk, they just shove some sort of malted drink at us. And how are they supposed to grow on that? "It's children we're talking about!" I say to them. "They have to grow!" And they say: "We all have our problems." Bah! Let them choke on their problems! I'm all on my own here, no assistants. I'm going right out of my mind and into the mental hospital to join the souls of Charcot.'

I said nothing. It was all true. I should go.

'You won't see it my way. Well, all right, I'll take you. It's a fixed post you see, and I don't want a goat for that post.'

It was an odd sort of job, this fixed post. Why did it exist in the first place? It was a mystery. But then I suppose it was quite sensible – although war raged and there wasn't enough of anything, not enough milk nor enough bread, there was always music. Flow on little stream of culture, created by someone long ago, flow on and help people to live.

The House of the Child even contained a grand piano, old and badly out of tune, but with traces of a pure and noble tone. I set to work. First I had to call in the tuner. I had a battle over this with our directress, Eulampia Zakharovna: the sound was perfectly adequate in her opinion. But I crushed her with my authority and invoked my specialist education. (In general I hardly ever referred to it.) A tuner was eventually found, a cobwebby old man, very garrulous, who kept asking: 'Do you recognise me?' when he meant 'Do you understand me?' It was rather hard to 'recognise' him as his thoughts were so confused, but one thing was clear: he demanded a 'wee bottle' for his work. Another battle with Eulampia Zakharovna who wanted to give him not a full bottle but a quarter-litre one. The old man was adamant, and within a week the directress had given in. Where she got the bottle was not clear. That woman was an absolute genius at getting hold of things and could beg, barter or buy absolutely anything. 'I'd have gone far if only I'd known arithmetic!' she said. So the piano was tuned and I anxiously sat down to play it. My hands, my hands! But they obeyed, with difficulty, and I managed to play a few little songs from Tchaikovsky's *Children's Album*. Once, long ago, I had practised these pieces seated at the piano with a ribbon in my plait, dreaming of freedom, the courtyard and 'cossacks and robbers', and they had forced me to sit down and play. I hated music then, as though I had a premonition that I'd never be any good at it . . . 'The Doll's Illness', 'The Doll's Funeral'.

'It's alright for an invalid,' said the directress. 'I've heard worse.'

'Can you do "Katyusha?"' asked Nyura, the full-faced technician who had waved her bucket at me on that first day. 'I adore "Katyusha". I cry every time I hear it.'

I managed to pick out 'Katyusha' by ear. Nyura burst into tears.

'What does education matter?' she said, drying her tears. 'If I have a son I'm definitely going to send him to the conservatoire.'

So started my second musical life. In some ways it was more successful than the first. Gradually, day by day, I became more fluent, more daring. I not only played – I sang! I drew all the children's songs from the same place – from the depths of my childhood days when I wore a ribbon in my plait. My nurse sang me this song, my mother that one.

I'd never realised how much little children needed music! They drank it in, like the dry earth soaks up water. Even the youngest ones, the babes in arms. When the babies had their music hour, their high white iron cots, neatly made up, would be wheeled into the hall where the piano stood. They'd all be crying and complaining of their fate, but the moment I started to play they'd quieten down and listen. Their milky blue eyes would stare vaguely, mysteriously, observing something completely inaccessible to the rest of us, possibly something to be found behind the backs of our heads. Some of them would raise their tiny hands, with little rays of fingers, and seem to beat time. The older ones, the crawlers and toddlers, understood even more. They would stand up in their playpens on weak, bowed little legs which couldn't yet walk, and would clutch the rails as though reaching out for the song. The best thing of all was when they all shyly sang together, in droning tuneless voices. The toddlers' singing always touched me – I won't say to tears, because I had no tears left, but to a lacerating tremor of sadness. And those who were slightly older still and could walk, the one-and-a-half to two-year-olds, how eagerly they crowded round the piano! The children were pale and rickety, their little legs were all crooked, many of them were quite backward compared to children living at home, many of them hadn't yet learned to speak and communicated in signs and twitterings. But in this room they livened up and squealed for joy, each one trying to get a bit closer and grabbing my dress. One of them, bolder and more grown-up might even reach out to the piano and touch a note. 'Music,' I would say, and they would babble the difficult word after me. Music was a miracle for them, and it was indeed a miracle. The grand piano groaned, my cramped hands lumbered about the keys – yet it was still music, as though it wasn't me playing but music itself, magnanimously forgiving me for my clumsiness.

They gradually got used to me at the House of the Child. I helped Eulampia Zakharovna with her arithmetic – we got on splendidly together – and sometimes I would stay behind after work and accompany the cooks and childminders in a sing-song. Nyura had a lovely voice, more like a bell. It didn't merely distinguish itself from the rest, it reigned supreme, providing a Herculean background for the others. 'You should take lessons Nyura!' we'd say, but she'd just wave her hand. She dreamed of going off to the front, or at least working in an armaments factory, but she stayed on out of pity for the children and the directress whom she couldn't bear but loved all the same. This Nyura had a really paradoxical nature: passionately law-abiding yet contemptuous of the law, unmarried yet determined to bear a son: 'I'll just meet someone and have a baby with him,' she'd say.

All in all, then, I was delighted with my job. My wages were low, less than a technician's, but they were enough for me. My job entitled me to be fed, and I would take a tin of soup home every day.

[3]

Home . . .

Work is one thing, but we all need a home to go back to where we can take off our working clothes, put on a dressing-gown and live.

The flat was in a large, gloomy, six-storey building

constructed some time around the turn of the century with various unsuccessful attempts at the modern style, all twists and curlicues, with lilies on the facade. Now it was run down, peeling and dilapidated: the lift didn't work, the plaster was falling off and the courtyard was littered with the debris of the lilies. There were four rooms in the flat besides mine: three women lived in three of them, one in each room, and the fourth was locked while its owners, Fyodor and Anfisa Gromov, were away at the front.

These were my neighbours in the flat, and with these people I was destined to live. They're my family now – formed not by choice but by chance. Before, people used to get married not by choice but by the match-makers, and they lived to tell the tale. So for me, doubly bereft, this was the only possible form of the family now, and if this hadn't existed I wouldn't have been able to bear it.

My neighbours then were Kapa Gushchina, Pavla Zykova (we all called her Panka) and Ada Efimovna. I can see them all as they were when I first met them: not old, but not so young either. Many years have passed since then, and we've all changed of course, but I don't notice many changes and to me we all seem exactly the same now as we were then – not old but not so young either. Kapa's smooth black hair is just the same (although there are a few streaks of grey now); Ada's graceful legs are as slender as ever. I think Zykova has grown even skinnier with the years and there's more grey straw now in her permed hair, but she's still as rough and energetic, and still stands up for the truth as she sees it.

Kapa Gushchina (Kapitolina Vasilevna Gushchina to be precise) worked then as a night watch. (She has since retired and is now living on a pension.) Small and plump with wide hips, like a chess piece, she walks smoothly and inaudibly in her cloth slippers. She doesn't recognise the fashions and always wears several skirts reaching almost to the ground – maybe because she has crooked legs. Her face, however, is pretty and apple-like. She pronounces her 'o's very strongly and is very religious: she loves the church and everything religious – funerals, weddings and christenings. She dreams of entering a convent in her old age. 'But there aren't any left now,' she complains. 'They've all been destroyed, like bed bugs with powder.' She was married twice and both her husbands died.

Ada Efimovna is a former operetta singer. She lost her voice long ago and left the stage, but remained devoted to her art all her life and got a job selling tickets just so as not to have to leave the theatre with its bright lights and velvet. Her stage name was Ulskaya but in her passport it is Zayats; she loathes this rather unbecoming name and still blushes when the postman brings her her pension and she has to sign for it. In fact, she is quite ugly, with a squashed nose and soft bulging cheeks, but there is undoubtedly a certain devil-may-care look about her, with her fluttering scarf, her crooked little finger and her flowing skirts. She always refers to herself in diminutives: 'my little head is aching', 'my little hands are frozen'. She has a guttural voice with a slight speech defect like a lark's trill, and she not only burrs her 'r's, she lisps – 'sweet' is 'thweet', but with such a soft, aspirated 'th'. She is sentimental, kind and absurd. She laughs as though she is being tickled with her consent, and when she does so her eyes become like slits and almost disappear. She was married three times: her third husband (I think he was Zayats) died; the other two are still alive and are singers.

In the room furthest from the hall door, darker and uglier than the others (probably the servants' room) lives Panka Zykova, Panka the fitter, then and now a fitter, and surely a fitter to the end of her days. Time will never change her. A tall mannish woman, all rough joints, she seems to have not two knees but ten. When she walks into the room there's a gust of wind. She is fierce and honest, she doesn't like strangers, and she'll never yield her rights. She hated me at first sight, but there was something passionate and honest in that hatred that was far more appealing then mere indifference. She was married once but her husband died. Panka doesn't like talking about herself, and one learns about her from others, mainly from Kapa, who knows everything.

When I had just moved into the flat and hadn't yet got to know any of the others properly, Kapa Gushchina asked me: 'Have you a husband?'

'He died at the front.'

'So you're a widow?'

'That's right.'

Kapa hummed mockingly, but with a certain satisfaction: 'Congratulations! So they've sent us another one. Now we have a full crew – a widow in every room. This isn't a flat, it's a ship of widows!'

'A ship of widows,' I repeated when I returned to my room. There was something quite magical about these words, a sort of unhurried, lumbering motion. I often couldn't sleep at night and would look through my bare window at the rain or snow. All year round there was a lantern hanging there casting a long shadow, and I felt as though our ship of widows with its crew was sailing through the ages to some unknown destination.

Many years have passed and we are all still sailing on in our ship of widows.

* *

Living for such a long time in such close quarters to one another, it's impossible to remain strangers, and strangers we are certainly not. There always arises a particular sense of kinship amongst neighbours. They quarrel, they insult one another, they vent their nervous rage on one another, yet despite everything they're a family. When you fall ill your neighbours do the shopping, bring it to you, make tea. When you die they bury you, pray for you, drink to you.

I know so much about each of my neighbours that it's as though they were transparent, as though their souls were visible through their bodies. I am not sure now how I came to know so much about them – whether they told me about themselves, or whether other people did, or whether I just imagined it all. But one way or another, I can see each one of them with penetrating clarity, both their public and their private faces. As to the second, though, I'm generally wrong: one's inner world is always so much more complicated than anyone else could possibly imagine. But I try. I have this persistent desire to migrate into other people. Sometimes I feel as though I have lost my own eyes and am merely looking at the world through those of the others – first Kapa's, then Panka's, then Ada Efimovna's little slits. But more often with the grey eyes of Anfisa, whom I loved more than all the others. Anfisa Gromova was like a sister to me, God-given, fate-given, even though we quarrelled cruelly and would be sworn enemies for days on end. Now she has died, leaving the rest of us to survive her. I know I'm not really to blame for her death, yet I cannot stop blaming myself for it.

Anfisa Gromova wasn't with us then. She returned from the front in the autumn of forty-three.

I can see it all – with that tormenting clarity borrowed from others, which may well be mistaken.

It is a dreary, wet autumn day. Anfisa, looking huge in her long mud-spattered greatcoat, is standing at the doorway to the building. From under an absurd little forage cap her straight wet hair straggles across her cheeks. The kit-bag over her shoulder makes her look bent and old. She dithers at the doorway, staring at the sparrows calmly hopping about in the puddles and feels so sorry for them – they look just like sick children. The vast, dirty yellow, peeling building seems so strange to her now, as though she'd never lived here before. Having stood at the doorway for a while pitying the sparrows –

just to gain time – she sighs, pushes the door, which opens with a groan, and makes her way up the stairs. She walks as painfully and slowly as an old woman. The straps of her kit-bag cut into her shoulders, especially the left one, near the collar-bone, where she was wounded the previous year. She stops on the landing and sighs again.

She has come home.

[4]

Standing on the third-floor landing in front of her own door, Anfisa both recognised it and didn't recognise it. The letter-box looked new, with a lock on it that hadn't been there in her time. And there was a new list of tenants tacked to it. Ring once for Zykova, twice for Gushchina, three times for Ulskaya, four times for Flerova. Anfisa hadn't known any Flerova and wondered anxiously whether this meant they'd given away her room. She rang twice, for Gushchina. No answer. She rang twice again. There was a rustle at the door, the chain jangled and a familiar voice asked: 'Who is it?'

'One of us,' said Anfisa.

'What do you mean "one of us?" It's all very well, but nowadays they'll steal your coat before you know it!'

'So that's how these civilians live now, they all distrust one another,' thought Anfisa. 'I prefer it at the front.'

'Open up Kapa, it's me!'

The door opened a crack and a familiar black eye appeared.

'Don't you recognise me?'

'Oh Lord, Fiska!' Kapa gasped, and flung open the door. 'I didn't know who you were at first. You look terrible, don't be cross with me but you look terrible.' Kapa herself hadn't changed at all; she was just as sleek as ever. They were obviously lying when they said how bad civilian life was.

'So you've come back, lost one. Why didn't you write? We'd given you up for dead.'

'Well I'm not.'

'Well, well. You're alive, so come in. What's brought you back? No more fighting?'

'No, no more fighting,' said Anfisa quietly, stepping over the doorway. Lifting the straps of her heavy wet kit-bag she took it off and put it on the floor.

The entrance hall was in darkness – maybe Kapa hadn't noticed yet? She must have done. Kapa noticed everything! Her bright black eyes soon found what they were looking for – Anfisa's stomach, on which her greatcoat was all bunched up and the buttons didn't meet. Kapa beamed, as though she'd been rubbed in butter. 'And with a little present too. Congratulations, dear, and best wishes!' Anfisa said nothing. 'So fate threw you and Fyodor together again, eh?' Anfisa shook her head. 'Well well, so the wind blew. It does happen . . .'

'Don't Kapa, don't ask me about it now. I haven't the strength. I'm wet and dog-tired, my kit-bag's weighing me down and I've a wounded shoulder.'

'What's in your kit-bag?'

'Oh, this and that – food concentrates, tobacco, tins of "Second Front" stewed meat . . . '

'Can I have a tin of "Second Front"?'

'You can have two, just let me unpack first. Now where's the key to my room? Have you got it?'

'I have indeed!' Anfisa felt greatly relieved. So they hadn't given away her room after all! 'When I saw O.I. Flerova on the door I thought you'd given my room away and my heart was in my mouth,' she said.

'God save us, would I do a thing like that?'

'So who's this Flerova?'

'Lord, I don't know. She's a widow. They sent her to replace the Makoshins. Bad case of nerves, a bit of an intellectual. She's got a radio in there and listens to it. And what do they play on it? Nothing but buzzing and humming if you ask me. Now if it was the Pyatnitsky choir or some funny songs I wouldn't mind so much, but all she ever listens to is that awful wailing noise – a violin maybe, or an accordion or some such thing, ugh! Panka Zykova just hates it but it doesn't worry me. What do I care? Let her listen to it, as far as I'm concerned. All people are good, that's what I say!'

'You've got the key, have you? I'd like it . . .'

'Don't worry, your key's here, and your room and all your things. I haven't touched a button. I'm not a thief. I respect God. You people have all forgotten God, that's why he punished you and sent you this war. There's a new priest at the Elokhovskaya church and he says so: "to each according to his deeds . . . " '

'I'd like my key Kapa, I'm tired.'

'Wait a bit, don't rush, don't worry. I haven't moved so much as a speck of dust, everything's in its place, your clothes are all hanging there, and your overcoat. Toska the janitor kept going on at me: "Sell it to me, sell it to me," she says. "Fiska was killed long ago," she says. "The rain's washing my bones clean and there you are guarding her property like Koshchei the immortal guarding over death." "No," I say, "I shan't sell it to you. Fiska will be back." And I was right. All right I'll bring it, I'll bring it . . .'

Kapa brought the key and opened the door. The room smelt of mice. For Anfisa it was a painful sight: dirt, dust, peeling wallpaper . . . Fyodor's Sunday trousers, pure wool, hung on the wall, probably all moth-eaten by now. On the bed were scattered some pillows in dirty pillow-slips. 'Who stayed here while I was away?' demanded Anfisa.

'Who would have stayed here? No one stayed here.

Panka Zykova will complain to you that I let people sleep here for money, but don't you believe her, she's lying like a snake. She has such a long tongue it gets tangled up in her legs. I only let them here twice, and that wasn't for money but out of the goodness of my heart. Such a nice little couple they were too, like two turtle doves. So I let them stay. I don't need people's money; if they bring me some foodstuffs then I'll take it so as not to cause offence. But all your things are here, look and see for yourself.'

'Did he wear Fyodor's trousers? They're hanging on the wall and I left them in the cupboard in mothballs.'

'I don't know anything about the trousers. Such a nice little couple they were. He needed your trousers like a priest needs a rubber ball. Elegantly dressed, smart tie, army jacket. And she had long, long curls all over her shoulders . . .'

Anfisa wasn't listening. She was looking at her plants. She had kept a lot of plants and flowers once. They'd been the best in the whole house. Now there were just some withered budleia in jamjars. She felt so sorry for the flowers, more sorry than anything. 'You promised to water them, Kapa.'

'I know, I'm sorry, I just didn't have time. You rush about all day from one queue to another, and there's nothing to cook, and then you have all the washing to do – and the days fly past. And at night I have to work. But don't you feel sorry about your little flowers dear – it's people you should feel sorry for, not flowers.'

'I don't mind.'

'What d'you mean you don't mind. I can see how upset you are.'

'I'm not upset, just tired.'

'Well, have a rest, and Christ be with you.'

She went out and Anfisa dragged off her hard wet coat (it seemed as though it would stand up on its own), then set to work on her tarpaulin boots (size 43). As she pulled them off she sighed, as though she'd just run a great distance. She unwound her footcloths, then sat down to get her breath back. She put her large bare feet with their crooked toes onto the floor, moved her knees apart slightly and rested her large clumsy stomach on them. Inside her stomach the baby romped and kicked, sticking something sharp into her ribs – an elbow maybe, or a knee. You could see him sticking out, even under her field shirt. Anfisa broke into a smile, as she always did when her son – she knew she was going to have a son – was particularly lively. His silent mobile life, subservient to no one, filled her with tenderness. 'He wants to come out, my sweet one.' The baby kicked and kicked, shifted the angular part from her rib and grew quiet. Anfisa too grew quiet. There was a knock at the door. It was Kapa again.

'Listen Fisa, why don't you give me that green cardigan to keep for you. You don't need it now, but I have to go to church. The nights I stayed awake watching your property!'

'All right, you take it.'

'It's only fair. I don't want to take other people's things. Your bucket's in the kitchen, I don't do my washing in it, even though Panka Zykova does. "This bucket is now communal property," she says, "since its owner has been killed." She has no shame. So she sticks her bottom up and she washes. In someone else's bucket too.'

'It doesn't bother me, let her wash in it.'

'What's more, she's moved a demobilised peasant in with her for her sinful flesh, and he's living here unregistered. In the mornings he has a good long wash, fills the sink with spit, sits in the latrine all morning with a cigarette . . .'

'What do I care? Let him sit there.'

'You let them do this and you let them do that, and one day you let them do it once too often.'

'Kapa . . .'

'I'll say no more. I didn't say anything. I mean no

harm. Everything's all right with me, just so long as it's all for the best. I only want to help and understand. Look at you sitting there with no shoes on, and the floor's so cold! D'you want to catch a female inflammation? Put your shoes on at once, then sit down. Shall I put the kettle on for you?'

'Thanks Kapa, I'll do it.'

'You've come back terribly cultured. Higher education! I shan't bother you any more. Adieu.' Kapa went out. She was offended. Anfisa sat there with her bare feet on the bare floor (there was something so pleasant about the cold), and pondered. She'd been longing to think things over for so long now, but there'd been no time to on the train . . .

[5]

What of her husband, Fyodor?

Before their marriage she and Fyodor had worked together at the same factory, she as a storekeeper, he as a moulder. It was a rare speciality in those days, and in short supply, so Fyodor was a highly valued worker. He was also a great shock-worker. They got to know one another at their amateur talent club. There was a women's choir at the factory called the Snowflakes. The managers splashed out and dressed the whole choir in white floor-length satin gowns. They looked really beautiful all standing in a semi-circle, dazzling white and sparkling. Anfisa sang in this choir. She had a strong, pure voice although it was somewhat thick – an alto they called it. The conductor preferred the altos to the sopranos: sopranos were two a penny at the factory but altos were few and far between.

Fyodor played solo guitar. That's how they got to know one another – better and better as time went on. He began to woo her and it became obvious that he was serious. He had three dances with her – a pas d'espagne, a waltz and a polka coquette – then said straight out: marry me. Anfisa had nothing against Fyodor, she liked him a lot in fact, but she was a bit bothered by the fact that he was younger than her – she was twenty-six and he was twenty-five. He was really very good-looking though: light as a feather, slightly shorter than her and narrower in the shoulders, but strong. He had fine, red curly hair, like a bonfire. Anfisa thought a bit, then accepted.

They got married and set up house together. The factory gave them a room, a good bright room, twenty metres. At their wedding, which was paid for by the factory, everyone shouted 'bitter!'* and did all the other things people do at weddings. Anfisa soon stopped working – it wasn't worth it, her wages were pitiful and if Fyodor was careful he could bring home twice as much. So she bustled about shopping and cleaning all day and kept everything spotless, and there'd still be time for her to listen to the radio when she'd finished, for she loved music. Fyodor would come home from the factory exhausted; he'd have a wash and brush his hair, then have his dinner which she'd always have waiting on the table for him. Fiery borsch with salt and pepper, or cabbage soup with pork. Fyodor didn't crave meat especially but he did like hot dishes. He'd finish eating, wipe his lips and kiss her: 'Hello my beauty!' Anfisa was certainly not a beauty, but she wasn't exactly a monster either: straight, strong and stately, with a light brown plait falling to below her waist. Fyodor loved it when she unloosed her plait in front of him and brushed it.

* It's the custom for guests at Russian weddings to shout 'bitter!' when the new husband and wife kiss, referring to the vodka on the man's breath.

Fyodor was a wonderful worker, both in the factory and at home. Soldering, repairing, painting – he did everything. They respected him in the flat. Even Panka Zykova, always complaining about something, was embarassed to do so in his presence. A sharp knife was music to her ears, and she didn't argue when Fyodor was at home. Anfisa and Fyodor used to sing various songs from films, the radio and the amateur talent club, he taking the soprano part, she the alto. They were particularly successful with a shepherd and shepherdess duet: 'My dear little friend'. They sang old folk songs too, which Anfisa's grandmother had taught her. Anfisa had had a hard childhood: she'd been brought up in the country and poverty had made her mother spiteful, but her grandmother was wonderful. She sang well, and had passed it on to Anfisa. This was good for family life.

Fyodor wasn't a big drinker. He hardly drank at all in fact, even on Mayday or the anniversary of the Revolution, and if he did he never acted up. He'd just say: 'I've had too much, Fisa,' and go straight to bed. Next morning he'd wake up and say: 'Forgive me for yesterday.' But what was there to forgive? He was only a man after all.

Anfisa's father, it could be said, was never really dry. But this man got drunk once in a lifetime. She'd give him a little glass of vodka to sober him up, and he'd soon be all right.

They had a good life, it couldn't be denied. There was just one thing – they had no children. Anfisa loved babies; at first she hoped to have her own, but at last she stopped hoping. There was nothing to be done about it: she was infertile. Fyodor was like her child, with his blue eyes and curly hair. In recent years he had begun to go bald on top. He was mortified: 'You won't love me when I'm bald,' he said.

'But I like you bald just as much,' she said. 'Besides, does happiness depend on whether you've got hair or not?'

They lived so peacefully together. They would go to bed at night, the bedspread clean and cool, the pillows soft as swans, the alarm clock ticking: 'I'm here, I'm here,' and Anfisa would put her arms round Fyodor's neck and lay his heavy man's head on her shoulder, and she would feel so happy! She would listen to Fyodor sleeping for a while, then fall asleep herself.

They lived together happily like this for eight years, then suddenly it was war! Fyodor immediately received his call-up papers. Anfisa collected them and wept, and that evening they all sat round the table together seeing the soldier off to war. Kapa had a bit of vodka to drink and was soon wailing for Fyodor as though he'd died already. Anfisa didn't howl: she didn't know how to wail like a peasant woman, yet was ashamed that she didn't have a really good cry like Kapa.

Next morning Fyodor got up, washed, ate, buckled on his belt – and said goodbye. Anfisa clutched him to her breast and he couldn't tear himself away from her. At last he gently pushed her aside. 'Now now,' he said, 'we're not saying goodbye forever, they may not kill me. Wait for me.' And off he went. It was as though he'd vanished off the face of the earth – no letters, not so much as a postcard. Anfisa was all on her own then; she became more and more depressed and gloomy as though the light had gone out of her life. She went to the factory and asked them to take her back, and they gave her a job on the shopfloor – they badly needed the workers. But now everything was different at the factory: the men had all been taken off, there were only women left now and the lads from the factory-school and old Kuzmich, the foreman, who looked like Moroz.* Anfisa worked conscientiously, but the boredom and depression didn't go. She felt she had nothing to live for. She didn't cook dinner

*Father Frost.

any more, she just kept going on cold scraps. She still washed though, but it was almost unconsciously, like a cat scraping its paws over its face. At night she was disturbed by her alarm clock and slept badly. She grew thin and ugly. And still there were no letters. She waited and waited, patiently and uncomplainingly, then she decided to leave for the front to see Fyodor. Where he was fighting she didn't know, but she'd be nearer to him at the front, and who knows, they might even meet there.

So she enrolled in a nursing course. She was the oldest there: the others were all young girls, and she was thirty-five. She worked all right and was good at practical things, but she was no good at theory. They didn't insist on that though, they were more interested in practice. She finished the course and was given an assignment. It was all one to her where she went since she didn't know where Fyodor was. She only asked to be near the front line of battle, and they agreed. If she'd known how it would be she'd never have volunteered to go there – but it was too late, there was work to be done. Anfisa worked as conscientiously as ever, although she was a dreadful coward and the bombs terrified her, worse than wolves. She wasn't so afraid of the shooting. It was better if they came from the side than from above, although that was bad enough. Anfisa really hated the bombs, they made her quite sick; she once saw an unexploded bomb and it reminded her of a pig.

When the bombing started she'd always try to bury her head in something, under her bunk if she was on her bunk, under the table if she was sitting at the table. She'd put her head down and stick her backside out, and her sisters and comrades would roar with laughter: 'Look out Fiska, it'll blow away your best feature!' Somehow she managed to get used to it though, she overcame her cowardice and worked no worse than the others. The main thing was that the patients liked her; she had a good effect on them and knew how to soothe and cajole them, even though she was such a coward. She was big and strong, and could lift anyone, so they called her Fiska the Crane. She had to cut off her plait as it wouldn't fit under her forage cap and it was a bother to wash: water was in short supply and they didn't get more than a teapot-full a day. She was afraid that Fyodor wouldn't love her any more without her plait, but she looked all right with short hair. She didn't look at herself much in the mirror, but the girls told her not to worry and said it was only decent after all for such an old woman. And one wounded lieutenant even fell in love with her! A pale and sickly fellow with an Adam's apple sticking out like the wing of a wounded chicken. 'Water!' he cried to her once, delirious with fever, and she went to him and gave him a drink, and he said: 'Anfisa Maximovna, I've fallen in love with you!' What a joke – fallen in love with her indeed! Why she could have been his mother! But she didn't let on and didn't laugh at him, just stroked him and combed his hair, and he went back to sleep. She thought he'd forgotten all about it, but he hadn't. Just before he was evacuated, all blue and transparent still, he again cried out: 'Fisochka I love you very much and dream of marrying you!' And by then his temperature was back to normal. What a funny fellow! Fiska lowered her eyes and said: 'I'm sorry, I can't. I'm already married.' It was as if they were in a play.

Other men pursued her too, not in so many words, but they did so nonetheless. They were so affectionate, so tender, these men. In battle they'd be heroes, striding off into unknown hells, but when they landed up in hospital they were so helpless! They were afraid of injections, they'd faint, they'd fuss like children. And they needed comforting like babies. Fisa understood this very well and they loved her for understanding – they certainly didn't love her for her youth or beauty.

When the hospital was evacuated in a bombing raid she

was wounded in the shoulder. Shooting, shouting, stretchers, bombs from the side, bombs from above, people going out of their minds, sheer hell. In her haste Anfisa didn't immediately notice that she'd been wounded; it wasn't at all painful at first, it was just as though someone had pushed her shoulder and called out to her. But then she did notice. Oh lord, the blood! It was all over her sleeve and down her front. Anfisa was terrified of blood, she never could get used to the sight of others', and now it was on her, dripping off her like a piglet. She gave a thin cry like a hare, squatted down on the ground and covered her face with her hands. They came and helped her to the car and she stumbled along, screwing up her face with fear and saying: 'Brothers! Brothers!' over and over again. They sat her in the car and she kept repeating: 'Brothers! Brothers!' just like a gramophone. She was very frightened indeed.

Later on, lying in her bunk, she was in pain all right. It was as painful as though the flesh were being torn from her shoulder. They operated and removed a fragment of shell, large and sharp, the size of a little finger. How terrible to think that had been lodged inside her. How had it not killed her? She carried it around for a long time in her bag, then lost it somewhere. She was sorry about that; she'd like to have shown it to Kapa, just to prove she really had been in the fighting and hadn't been playing at it.

Anfisa had to stay in bed after her injury. She recovered quickly, like a dog – dogs are always considered especially tenacious for some reason – and soon returned to the hospital. Not to lie in bed now but to work. At first she was scared of everything, terrified she might be wounded again. At every shot or shell-burst she'd panic, forget what she was doing and drop her sterile instruments. Then she got used to it: she was still afraid, but no more so than normal.

She hardly ever thought about Fyodor now, there was

no time. Sometimes when she was getting ready for bed in the evening she'd remember how they used to lie together side by side – him on the outside, her by the wall, his head resting on her shoulder, exactly where she'd been wounded. But during the day she didn't give too much thought to him – there was too much to do, and Anfisa couldn't work and think at the same time. For her it had to be either one thing or the other – working or thinking. She got terribly tired too, and she was good for nothing when she was tired. So gradually Fyodor was forgotten. She would recall parts of him – his eyes, his hands, his red hair – but he didn't take shape for her as a whole person. Maybe he'd been killed, maybe he was alive – you could never tell in the war. Anfisa hoped he was alive, because he'd said 'wait for me' and people don't say things like that lightly. So she waited conscientiously and wasn't tempted by anyone else, although there were certainly plenty who wanted her.

That was until Grigorii appeared. He totally bewitched her. He was convalescing when she met him; his leg was in plaster and he walked on crutches, but cheerfully, with a dance in his step. He'd sit down, his crutches beside him and his leg sticking out, and he'd boast about it: 'Look what a beauty! This leg of mine is beyond all price, it must be at least ten kilos. Come on girls, who's next for a poke?'

The girls laughed and Anfisa laughed too, although she found it more frightening than funny. He was such a good-looking young fellow, so dashing and elegant, with sharp ears and a curl on his forehead. He looked like a gypsy, a horse thief. Anfisa had seen men like him as a child; they'd gone from village to village and the old women always threatened the children by saying: 'I'll give you to the gypsies!' Someone like this would wind you round his little finger in an instant, and before Grigorii had addressed so much as a word to her she sensed he was doing just that.

Once the other girls had gone off to a dance leaving them alone together, and Grigorii said: 'Hey there Fisa Fisochka! I like you a lot, better than all the others, in fact!'

Her heart sank – he was twisting her round his little finger all right. 'You look like a horse,' he said. 'And I love horses. Such kind animals, they stand there munching hay with their big intelligent eyes. You harness them up and they take you for a ride. Just like you.'

So he was a horse thief! Anfisa struggled with all her might to resist him, but in the end all she could say, in a quiet little voice, was: 'But maybe you've got a wife?'

'Sure I have! So has everyone, nothing special about a wife!'

'And children?'

'No children yet, I can't tell a lie. Unless she's conceived some without me. Such things do happen!'

'Don't you mind?'

'Why should I mind? I'm a strong lad, I can stand up for myself. I'm a cheerful sort of chap and I like to see everyone else cheerful too. "Wait for me!"' he mimicked, grimacing gleefully and swearing. 'That's for your "waiting". She waits and she waits and grieves and snivels – and meanwhile, would you believe it, I've gone and got myself killed! Oh-oh-oh, what a crying shame! No, let's all be happy as long as we live! Her, me, and you, Fisa.'

Then he embraced Anfisa with one arm – holding onto his crutch with the other – and that strong, iron arm of his squeezed her like a hoop. She put both her arms round him but she didn't yield to him at once. Yet it all seemed so simple: I'm happy, you're happy, he's happy. The new moon shining through the window over her left wounded shoulder turned, fell and tumbled out of the sky.

That's how their love affair started. They'd meet in the treatment room after that, stealing in there in the evenings for brief, passionate encounters. And it was there that Anfisa first discovered what love was. She used to think she loved Fyodor – little did she know then! There was simply no comparison. This affair with Grigorii was the real thing; everything was new and special, the whole world changed, the moon through the window wasn't a moon but a white flower, and their urgent breathing in the darkness didn't belong to anyone! The treatment room smelt of tar from Vishnevsky ointment, and this smell affected Anfisa like valerian affects a cat.

Love changed her; she grew prettier, she had black circles under her eyes and there was a certain wild quality in her face. The girls all noticed and giggled – but she didn't care. She wasn't even afraid of the bombing now.

Then Grigorii had his plaster removed and it was time for him to go back to his unit. It hit Anfisa hard when she realised that they'd have to part. It shook her badly: 'I can't live without you,' she said. 'I shall die without you.'

'No you won't. You're not the first and you're not the last. Don't be sad, Fisa Fisochka, bring up the rear with a pistol!'

'But I love you, Grisha!'

'Well, I love you too, but so what? You women! It's lovely to kiss you, but there's nothing worse than having to say goodbye to you! I even wrote a poem about it!'

And so he left. He didn't leave an address and he didn't promise to write either. And nothing remained of him, not even a snapshot.

What could she do? She went on living and working as before, but without feeling anything – her soul had turned to stone, and her life was as unreal as a dream. And her dreams were just as unreal. She'd dream that Grigorii came to her, tapping his crutches and wanting to kiss her, but just as the dream was ending she'd wake up in tears. Once he came to her all in black and said: 'I've been killed, Fisa,' and she shrieked out in a wild voice so that all the girls in the adjacent bunks woke up and rushed over to see what the matter was. She just lay there trembling and gulped down a glass of valerian. She cried all that day, to the detriment of her work, of course, so that the doctor even had to hush her up. But next night Grigorii came again, hobbling cheerfully on his crutches and completely alive. 'I told a lie,' he said. 'They didn't kill me after all.'

Then they kissed, and they kissed each other into oblivion until it all came to an end again.

So she lived, between dreams. Three months passed.

One night Grigorii went away, leaving her as usual with a beating heart and wet eyes. She lay there thinking and suddenly felt a little live thing fluttering deep in her stomach. She used sometimes to have a twitch in her cheek – it was just like that. She didn't pay any attention to it. So many things like that are of nervous origin.

Another time the little live thing moved not at night but during the day. She was taking some bandages somewhere and it jumped! Then Anfisa understood and turned cold. It couldn't be! Yet she knew it was: this little creature was hers. But she just had to have it confirmed, so she went to the treatment room, looking like nothing on earth and terrifying all the girls out of their wits. What a business! It couldn't be true – she was infertile!

A week passed, and now there was no longer any doubt about it: the little live thing was there, kicking and thumping and rejoicing and growing. He was happy, but for her it was death. It wasn't visible yet, thank god, but whatever would she do with herself when they found out?

It became visible soon enough though. One day she was washing in the bath-house with the girls and Klava the nurse said: 'So you're in the family way, Auntie Fisa!' Anfisa's mind went a blank – what could she say?

Klava broadcast the news round the whole hospital of

course, and people started looking at Anfisa and laughing. She could have died. She thought she'd never live it down, and even got hold of some pills to kill herself with. But it really wasn't so bad after all. People laughed, but not very much, and without any real malice. These things happen after all; they'd just have to send her back to the home front. True, the chief surgeon was furious: it was a frantically busy time, and Anfisa was his best nurse. 'You've cut off my right hand, d'you understand you stupid woman?' he shouted. But then he quietened down and forgave her. And the others weren't angry with her at all, and sympathised with her. The same Klava the liar did all her heavy work for her, and they didn't give her any heavy patients to lift. Everyone was so kind. No one so much as mentioned her husband Fyodor, and they hardly spoke of Grigorii at all; they gossiped a bit, but soon stopped. Anfisa had simply got herself in the family way and now had to go through with it and give birth. So she threw away her pills.

When her stomach had grown pretty big and everyone had got used to her condition she was summoned to see Vasilii Sergeevich, the political organiser. He was a stern man. She went in pale and trembling – this was it, it was all over for her now. 'What about your living husband then, Gromova?' he'd say. 'He spills his blood while you . . .' But he said nothing of the kind.

'So what's going on, Gromova? Who did it?'

Anfisa said nothing, and he repeated. 'Don't be shy, Gromova, tell me who it was. Maybe we can get you a reference. You're a serious woman, you wouldn't fall for just anyone . . . Tell me who it was.'

She didn't say anything. 'Well, don't tell me if you don't want to. We only want the best for you – you're an idol in skirts! Well, we shall have to send you home now, you know. Where are you from?'

'Moscow.'

'Ah, the capital of the world proletariat! Well, off you

go to swell the population of our capital city!'

Anfisa burst into tears.

'Don't be silly, I was only joking. Can't you take a joke? Eh, you women are a watery lot, however heroic you are. Give me your address.'

Anfisa scribbled her address in his notebook.

'Well, all the best to you my dear. Have a healthy child, but make sure he's a boy. So many of our men have been killed.'

Anfisa went on sobbing, smiling clumsily and promising to have a boy. She knew it would be a boy and had already chosen a lovely name for him – Vadim.

* *

She was sent off with some other pregnant women. They were well supplied: each of them had a kit-bag packed with foodstuffs, nappies and swaddling clothes. They were good people.

'Write and tell me how you get on, Gromova,' said the political organiser. 'And tell us if there's anything we can do to help.' And he kissed her like a brother. What a good man . . .

They were a long time on the train. The journey was endless. They kept uncoupling the engine and setting it on dangerous routes. The women waited, listened to the hooting, smoked and argued. Then they'd set off again and would all be friends until the train stopped yet again, and again they'd start arguing.

It was a long and difficult journey, but at last it ended and she got home. It was her home after all . . .

* *

Anfisa shifted her cold stiff foot on the floor. She sat and thought – she had her fill of thinking. Mainly she thought about Fyodor; she didn't decide anything for now. That would come later. Now it was time to tidy up. There were piles of dirt everywhere, she'd just have to sweep it all up. 'Arise, arise, it's a big country!' Anfisa said to herself, smiling at her own joke and getting up.

[6]

It was half-dark in the kitchen. The window looked out onto the blank back wall of the next-door house and the day was already coming to an end: these autumn days were so short. Two women stood by the stove. One, in a parrot-coloured dressing-gown, was Ada Efimovna, the other woman had a tortured face and was wearing a dark dress and a grey shawl; this must be Flerova, the new tenant. The women turned round to greet Anfisa when she came in; Ada apparently didn't recognise her at once.

'Hello Ada Efimovna, it's me, Anfisa.'

Ada clapped her hands, her sleeves billowing, and croaked hoarsely, as though there were peas in her throat: 'Anfisa! Lord, what a surprise! I never expected to see you! How wonderful!'

'I've come back here to live,' said Anfisa.

'Let me introduce myself,' said the dark woman. 'I'm Olga Ivanovna Flerova. And you must be Anfisa Maximovna if I'm not mistaken.'

Anfisa nodded and stretched out her hand. Flerova had a thin dark face with yellow patches under her eyes, like bruises which are just healing. She had uncombed, cropped hair, half grey and half black, falling in a fringe on her forehead, and intent blue eyes which questioned everything. Had she noticed?

Ada chirped hoarsely again: 'Oh Anfisa, you can't think how I grieved for you when we thought you'd been killed, and I'm so glad you weren't after all! I've got so much to tell you! I've had endless experiences in the realms of art, love and war!' She went up to Anfisa and kissed her with soft lips, then stepped back and screwed up her eyes. 'Well you certainly haven't grown any prettier. But what does it matter? We all lose our looks. That's life.'

'She hasn't noticed,' thought Anfisa.

'Now I'm relying on your support.' Ada hurried on. 'Gushchina has completely taken over here since you went away – she's been acting like a real dictator.'

Just as obsequious as ever – the war hadn't left any traces on her! Her hair was different though – some of it was yellow, some grey and some was green, like verdigris. Ada noticed Anfisa looking at her hair. 'Ersatz henna,' she explained. 'I was just experimenting. War's war, but you still have to look after yourself. You can't let yourself go for too long. But it all dried up and went green.' Flerova uttered a strange coughing sound from her throat. 'Don't you agree with me, Olga Ivanovna?'

'Oh yes, absolutely.'

'In fact a woman should take special care of herself in a war, both in her appearance and in her emotions. One should cultivate both art and nature . . . How about you Anfisa, do you look at the stars?'

Anfisa didn't know what to reply. What did she care about looking at the stars?

'It's a pity you don't then,' said Ada. 'I look at them constantly and it soothes my emotions. Sometimes I even cry. I'm such a little fool, such a child.'

'A child indeed!' mocked Kapa Gushchina, coming into the room. 'Why, you're almost a hundred, and you say you're still a child!'

Ada squeaked something and rushed to the door like a chicken fleeing a hawk.

'Barren fool,' said Kapa, 'Twitter twitter, jabber jabber . . .'

Flerova watched her closely with darkened face, then left the room.

'You saw that?' demanded Kapa. 'She stares and stares, and who knows what she sees? And she's so dark and thin – she's like something beyond the grave. People are right to say thin people can't be trusted. Fat people now, they're good and trustworthy, like me . . .'

The casserole Ada left on the stove started hissing, and its contents boiled up like a hat. Anfisa stretched out her hand to turn down the gas.

'Don't touch it!' shrieked Ada. 'She left it, let her look after it. Let it boil, let it burn, I'm not going to move a finger!'

'They're not getting on very well here,' Anfisa thought. 'It was better when Fyodor was here.'

She paled at the thought of her husband. She suddenly saw him standing before her in the kitchen, and it terrified her.

The door burst open and Panka Zykova entered like a gust of wind, bony, angular – just like a Nazi swastika, in fact. She confronted Anfisa, hands on hips, legs wide apart, and shouted: 'Now look here, you're not going to boil your baby clothes on the stove, d'you hear? I have to cook my dinner in here. I'm sorry but I'm not having her dirty baby clothes in here!'

Anfisa hadn't even made any baby clothes yet, and they were already telling her not to boil them . . . Kapa immediately took her side. 'And who said you could go round giving orders? We all live here you know, we're all the same, I don't care if she boils her baby clothes. And what's more you don't even pay your share of the gas!'

'I certainly do pay my share of the gas! We all pay equal shares, we all have one room!'

'But you should pay per person, not per room! Every person living here should pay! There's just one of me and one of Ada, but there's two of you, so you should pay for two!'

Panka gasped. 'Two? Who are you talking about?'

'Why Nikolai of course, your sweetheart!'

Panka spat and yelled at the top of her voice: 'Nikolai? What are you on about? He doesn't live here, why should I pay for him?'

'Hah! So he doesn't live here, does he? He only spends the day here, and spends the night here, and occupies the lavatory – and she says "He doesn't live here"!'

Panka's voice crescendoed to a high shriek; Kapa's too. Anfisa blinked. At last Kapa shouted: 'You won't get a brass kopeck out of me!' went out and banged the door.

Kapa, all puffed up after her shout, said: 'It's a great shame but she's not really a woman, she's a walking carbuncle. You must support me against her, Fisa. Then there'll be two of us and just one of her. That man isn't registered so he'll be afraid to poke his nose in. You boil your baby clothes, my dear, don't worry about her. A baby's a creature of God. We'll all pay for our light and gas per person and you and your baby will be two people, so you'll pay for two. It's only fair.'

Anfisa suddenly started sobbing loudly. 'I only came in here for my bucket, and you've started a whole bombing raid!' she said, blowing her nose on her apron. 'Where's my bucket?'

'Panka put it over there in the corner. "It's commmunal property now," she says. I say, nothing of the sort, not likely! Take it dear, don't worry, I'll support you.'

Anfisa ran some water into her bucket from the tap and went off to tidy up. She could have heated it on the stove but she wasn't used to hot water now. She scraped the floor with a knife and washed it, washed and polished the windows, tidied up, washed herself – and before she knew it the day was over. While she was working she forgot she hadn't eaten anything, and she wasn't particularly hungry either. To cook something would mean going into the kitchen again; Panka would come out and make a row, and Kapa too. 'Per person' indeed . . .! She'd rather eat a bit of bread here in her room instead. She got a half-eaten loaf out of her bag and ate it, washing it down with cold water. As she sat there the baby stirred in her stomach again, as though trying to get somewhere.

'Hush baby,' Anfisa said to him. 'We're home now, you'll soon be born.'

Anfisa lived very modestly as she waited for the birth; she economised on food and sold her greatcoat at the market. It wasn't as if she needed so much after all. She ate almost nothing now, not like in the old days – she'd had an appetite then, thank God, and could eat twice as much as Fyodor. She didn't make tea these days – Ada Efimovna would treat her. Ada was a good soul, even though somewhat operatic. She chattered away till your ears rang about love – how was it she didn't get bored by the same thing over and over again? She'd had three lovers in one year – and what was more, they were all called Boris! Anfisa couldn't believe she could have had so many all in one year. At least she should have had some shame.

Anfisa wasn't especially close to Flerova, until one day when she ran out of matches and didn't know where to get any. Ada had gone out, probably for a walk. So Anfisa knocked on Flerova's door.

'Can I come in, Olga Ivanovna?'

'Of course, Anfisa Maximovna.'

A polite person, and cultured. Kapa shouldn't have picked on her like that.

'I'd like to borrow some matches.'

'Please do, take the whole box if you want.'

'I only need to light the gas.'

'Take whatever you need. Why don't you sit down and have a chat?'

So they sat down together. Olga Ivanovna smoked a cigarette and tapped the ash constantly. But she looked all right really, not so old as she'd looked before, although her hair was grey and she had a twitching cheek. She smoked greedily, like a drunkard with a bottle. What do people get out of smoking like that? Anfisa had never developed the habit, even when she was a soldier at the front. The little room was bare and completely lacking in cosiness – just a chair, a table and a bookshelf. She lived poorly.

'How do you plan to live now?' Olga Ivanovna asked Anfisa. 'Will you work?' She asked her questions greedily, like she smoked.

'No, who'd take me now? Later on perhaps . . . ' She wanted to say 'when he's born', but was embarrassed.

'I'm constantly thinking about you,' said Olga Ivanovna. 'I work in the House of the Child you see – it's an orphans' home. They're terribly short of childminders, I know they'd take you. You could put the baby in the creche and work there yourself. How about it?'

She smiled, and took another cigarette. What a strange woman. Eccentric, but a dear. Anfisa felt as though they'd known each other a long time. She felt very comfortable with her – if only she wouldn't stare so.

She began visiting Olga Ivanovna regularly. She'd sit and chat for a while, then get up and go. Olga Ivanovna would offer her tea, and at first she'd always refuse – she hadn't come for that. But then she'd accept. (There was never anything to go with it.) Sometimes she'd ask for a book, which she'd read and return. The books weren't that interesting really, mainly translations and mainly about the past; they didn't touch Anfisa particularly. One book though she read avidly. It was called *The Insulted and the Oppressed*, it was about life and it was by Dostoevsky. She asked Olga Ivanovna whether she had any more by the same author, and Olga Ivanovna gave her *The Devils*. But she didn't like it. The characters said a lot of foolish things and committed murder too. She shouldn't read about such evil passions; it might damage the baby.

Sometimes Olga Ivanovna would turn on the radio and

listen to the latest news, or some music. Panka Zykova would fly into a rage over this music and throw things on the floor, but she had no authority to forbid it. So they'd listen to a symphony concert together. Anfisa only listened to be polite actually; symphony concerts tired her brain, she really preferred songs. Once she and Olga Ivanovna accompanied some songs on the radio, singing in a whisper so Panka wouldn't hear. It was funny – they were both so old to be behaving so young.

So gradually their friendship grew. Gradually Anfisa told Olga Ivanovna everything about herself – her life with Fyodor, the front, Grigorii, everything.

Ada Efimovna was jealous of Anfisa's friendship with Olga Ivanovna, and said Flerova had a cold reserved nature, lacking in love or inspiration. It was quite untrue, once you got to know her. But Ada really hadn't time to be very jealous, for she was just embarking on a new romance – her 'last love' she called it.

[7]

When Anfisa returned our flat became rather cosier, for me at least. Anfisa's eyes were a joy – grey, compassionate, radiating warmth and intelligence. But in general the atmosphere in the flat was tense and always on the verge of a crisis. There was always someone at war with someone – Kapa with Panka Zykova, Panka with Anfisa, Ada Efimovna with Kapa – and I was involved in various confrontations too, however sincerely I craved peace. It wasn't that there were any specially bad words said, everything depended on the tone of voice and the context. When I said to Kapa: 'You should be ashamed of yourself, Kapitolina Vasilevna!' I'm sure it wounded her far more than Panka's shrieking.

In these domestic battles coalitions and alliances were formed. The coalitions changed like patterns in a kaleidoscope, more often than not for unknown reasons. Sometimes everyone would take up arms against one person. And then there were dreadful periods when everyone was at war with everyone else. There were also periods when everyone was at peace with each other, but these were rare, and only in exceptional circumstances. These communal passions are often described as petty bourgeois. What rubbish! How could they be? They may be engendered by petty things but the passions themselves are lofty, noble – one might even say aristocratic. Each person fights for themselves, and for justice. And in this battle for justice people are prepared to sacrifice themselves and suffer, if only in order that evil may be punished. Whose fault is it if everyone has their own interpretation of justice?

So in our flat too, everyone wants justice done, but everyone understands the word differently. Everyone is just in their own way. One of the most painful things life has taught me is that each person is right in their own way. Even the scarecrow of the flat, Panka Zykova. A difficult person it must be said, yet she too is right in her own way.

It seems to me that Panka is a person possessed by passion, and this passion torments her, agonises her and makes her cry out loud. She passionately wants one thing: that everyone should be equal, that everyone should be like everyone else, and no one should be better than anyone else. And as this principle is constantly being violated she is constantly seething with rage. Why is Ada's room eighteen metres and bright, whereas Panka's is fourteen metres and dark? It's not right! Why is Gushchina's kitchen table by the window and brighter than the others? That's not right either! They should take Gushchina's table away from the window and put it in the corner. That would make it more cramped for me, but never mind, at least it would be fair!

Panka dreams of everyone being equal, if not equally happy then equally wretched. Maybe this idea took root in her in the years of war communism, when everyone was uniformly wretched. Panka despises us, her flatmates, in different ways. Ada Efimovna for her 'parasitism', for the fact that she has sung and danced her life away like the grasshopper, and has never been punished for it: and she gets a pension too! Me for my empty pretensions, for my radio, for the fact that I walk with a stick and 'demand pity', for the fact that when it's my turn to do the cleaning I don't wash the floor myself but pay Kapa to do it. It would be useless to explain to her that I'm an invalid and can't bend my back, that I'm simply incapable of washing the floor. 'You could if you had to!' she'd say. And maybe she'd be right too. I could if I had to. For Panka I'm a lady, and an impoverished lady at that, which is worst of all. Intellectual work she doesn't consider to be real work at all, and the fact that in our society it's generally better paid than physical work she considers an absolute scandal.

Kapa Gushchina she despises for her religion – peasant ignorance! Privately she considers her guilty of pilfering, and dreams of catching her red-handed, although she has never managed to do so. She avenges herself by all sorts of petty tricks – not calling her to the telephone and leaving the receiver off the hook, knocking her teapot off the stove and all but throwing it on the floor – why should it take up an extra burner?

Anfisa she despises for her woman's weakness: she got what she asked for. They all want it, you have to fight them off. Panka herself is really quite good natured, in a surly sort of way, and she's devoted to her husband, even if he isn't registered. What does it matter anyway? They don't sing songs, they don't have rows, they just sit quietly together in their room, drink a little vodka if there is any, then go to bed. And she's not going to pay per person, even if Kapa bursts a blood vessel trying to make her. There's no rule to say you have to.

I think Panka's anger is a result of the hard life she's had. It was a difficult and depressing life all right. She was orphaned early and fate didn't grant her beauty. It did give her a great height though, like a man, and what does a woman need that for? It's no use to her at all. Her first husband used to call her Ivan the Great. There were no children, he didn't want them; she had three abortions, then had gynaecological problems. Then her husband died of a bad liver – it was saturated with alcohol. He was a bad husband, yet he was her legal husband after all. Well, she had to survive him, so she got over it. A fitter's job is hard, man's work, and the pay is low. But Panka is proud and independent; she won't take tips and considers them to be bribes. We don't have tsarism any more, she said, and she's right . . .

But maybe it's not quite as simple as that. Possibly, even probably, Panka is more complicated than I've presented her. At all events she's a person.

Pondering on these domestic arguments I always come to the same conclusion: that everyone is right in their own way. I consider myself to be the least right of all. With my tiresome, or rather vicious habit of seeing things through other people's eyes, I can see myself from a distance, with the eyes of Kapa, Panka, even Ada Efimovna or Anfisa – although she's very fond of me on the whole – and I find many things about myself very irritating. I realise how irritating they must find my clumsy fingers, my bent back, my fixed stare, my habit of washing the cups with salt and soda instead of in the ordinary way . . . They are obviously right and I am generally wrong. But this recognition of their general rightness and my own wrongness doesn't make me any more pleasant. When they make fun of me and my rightness I snap at them, just like all the others.

[8]

It was soon time for Anfisa to have her baby. She went to the maternity home, where they praised her pelvis and told her not to worry – she'd deliver the baby as out of a cannon. And they gave her a date.

'But I'm thirty-seven already! D'you think I'll be all right?'

'Of course you will, dear,' said the doctor. 'What nonsense! Don't you dare think like that! Do some exercises.' And she gave Anfisa a book of exercises for pregnant women.

Anfisa started doing the exercises, but found them so funny that she gave them up. They must be for people who had nothing better to do. She started to await the date. And the date passed, and two weeks beyond the date, and still nothing happened. She waited some more, used up all her foodstuffs and still nothing happened. And her son grew quiet inside her: maybe he was dead! Lord save us!

Then Kapa suggested that she go to the bath-house and have a hot steam. Next morning Vadim asked to come out. Ada Efimovna took Anfisa to the maternity home (Olga Ivanovna was at work). They said goodbye at the door.

'Well, Christ be with you, as Kapa would say, although I don't believe in Him . . . But just in case . . . Motherhood is a great and wonderful thing.'

'Thank you for being so sweet,' said Anfisa, starting to cry. 'If something should go wrong forgive me for everything.'

'You mustn't cry at such a happy time. A new person's

about to be born! Maybe a great person!'

Anfisa went into the reception room. It was bright and frightening. There were posters depicting complicated births on the wall – facial presentations, breech births . . . Fancy putting them there! They laid her on a cold white trestle bed and examined her.

'Well, this one'll be quick – she's an elephant, not a woman!'

But elephant or no elephant, it wasn't quick at all! The pains simply went away and she lay there like a lump, unable to give birth and unable to go away. She'd have a few weak contractions, then they'd stop. This went on for two days and nights. And the baby didn't stir. 'He must have died,' Anfisa wept. 'And I'll die too.'

'You won't die,' they told her. 'Everything's normal, lie down.'

On the third day the doctor decided to induce her, and within twenty-four hours Vadim was born, weak, choking, and with a squashed head. 'The mountain's given birth to a mouse,' said the doctor.

Anfisa lay there weakly after the baby's cry, feeling as light as if they'd lifted a mountain off her.

'Well mother, you've got a boy.' A boy . . . She knew it would be. Was he alive? Why wasn't he crying?

'He was choking, they're resuscitating him,' said the woman on the next table. She was evidently between contractions, and licked her bitten lips.

Anfisa moved and wanted to cry out, but she'd lost her voice. In the corner they were doing something with her baby. She heard a baby's cry, but it was weak, like a little frog.

'Show me, show me!' wheezed Anfisa.

They showed her her baby from a distance. He was terrifying and tiny, and for some reason his little head kept flopping down. Then they took him away. Anfisa struggled and shouted: 'Give me my son! I haven't even seen him!'

No one payed her any attention – just rushed past her. 'Give me my son!' she shrieked, her voice fast returning. They hushed her up. 'Quiet now mother,' they tutted. 'They'll bring him for you to feed, you'll see him then.'

Anfisa didn't argue. She understood discipline – she'd been a nurse herself.

Soon they moved her to another ward. Time passed, but still they didn't bring her her son. So that was it, he'd died and they wouldn't tell her. All around her the other mothers were feeding, but they still didn't bring him to her. She couldn't bear it, and despite all her disciplined intentions she began to sob loudly. She sobbed and shouted: 'Give me my son! Give me my son!' And she banged her head against the iron bed.

'Hush! This isn't a market-place!' said a stern midwife. 'There are a hundred of you in here, and you're the only one making a fuss, Gromova!'

'My son!' Anfisa screamed. 'Give me my son this instant!'

'What's this?' said the stern midwife raising her voice. 'We're all working here and you howl like a pig! I shall call the chief doctor this instant!'

She went to the door and called: 'Vladimir Petrovich, come here a moment, Gromova is taking liberties!'

The doctor came, the same one who'd received her. His sleeves were rolled up, his spectacles were on his forehead and his face was angry. He looked severely at Anfisa and said: 'Stop acting like a hooligan!'

That frightened her, and she quietened down. She'd never been accused of hooliganism before. She decided she'd better keep quiet now.

That evening her temperature went up, not much, just 37.9 but still.

'It's your own fault for shouting like that,' said the stern midwife.

'Just give me my son,' said Anfisa.

'It's not allowed. Go to sleep mother.'

'I know he's died. Tell me, stop tormenting me.'

'Died? No one has died. Infant mortality is a thing of the past here. Go to sleep.'

Anfisa sank into oblivion. In a semi-delirium she imagined that the white wall of the ward was moving closer and closer, and that there behind the wall was her son, and they wouldn't let him come to her. Now he was already fully grown, standing on his own two feet and walking towards her, thump, thump, thump . . . But they wouldn't let him in to see her, and he was dying. Somewhere beside her they were digging a grave. 'Put me with my little boy, bury me beside my son,' Anfisa shouted with a superhuman effort, but no one was listening. And again the reality of the white wall, and behind the wall lay the baby, and the baby was being buried . . .

When she woke up it was bright daylight in the white ward, pillows of fresh snow lay outside the windows and sunbeams danced on the ceiling. All around her women were feeding their babies – little white bundles on white pillows. A midwife came in, not the stern one this time but a cheerful one with a bundled up baby on each arm which she handed to two women.

'What about mine?' demanded Anfisa. 'Where's mine?' Then she suddenly remembered that he'd been buried, and shouted: 'Have you buried him?'

'Why should we bury him? He's bellowing like a rooster,' said the cheerful one. 'Yours has the loudest voice in the whole nursery. He'll be a general. That's what we call him – General Gromov. I'll bring him, I'll bring him.'

She returned with two more bundles. One of them was bawling – that was Vadim. He had a tense, red, angry face, and he shifted his head from side to side, rooting blindly with his mouth wide open.

'Time to eat, Comrade General!' The midwife laid the baby on a pillow next to Anfisa. He bawled desperately, angrily, without tears. She thrust her breast at him but he wouldn't take it, he was too angry. He twisted his head, bumped her with his nose, then suddenly seized the nipple and started chewing with his toothless gums. The milk flowed. The baby gulped eagerly and noisily.

'He sucks well,' said the midwife approvingly, 'A real activist.'

The milk flowed abundantly, in a thick stream. The baby wrinkled his nose, spluttered, looked angry, lost the nipple, found it again and again started work, sucking and gulping.

Anfisa fed her son. She overflowed into him, her master. No one had ever mastered her like this, neither Fyodor nor Grigorii. No one but Vadim.

[9]

After a few days Anfisa was discharged. Ada Efimovna collected her, like a true comrade. She chirped, and was moved to tears by the baby's smallness. She spoke of the sanctity of motherhood.

'I never had that joy,' she said. 'Everything was for art and my figure. And what now? I've been torn from my art. I kept my figure I suppose, but what for? I have my figure, but no life.'

'That's quite true,' thought Anfisa. 'What's the point of a good figure when you've got no life?' But aloud she said hypocritically: 'Don't be sad, Ada Efimovna, no one ever knows how their fate will turn out.'

Vadim yelled. 'Lovely baby,' said Ada, peeping through a gap in the blanket. 'Very original colouring. But why does he scream so much? It makes me feel quite faint.'

They arrived home. Only Kapa was there.

'Well, show him to me then.'
Anfisa showed him.
'Unwrap him.' She unwrapped him. Vadim squirmed and bawled and twisted his little red legs.
'He's all right, a fine baby, beetroot coloured,' Kapa said approvingly. 'And a beetroot's better than a turnip. A turnip baby is bound to have a bad life. But your baby – his hands and feet and everything else are in the right place and he bawls good and loud – a real jazzer. We'll be having a lot of noise from him. I don't mind, but Panka will be on at you about the noise.'
'But he's only a baby, she'll have to understand.'
'Well, I didn't say he was a cat, did I? I know he's a baby.' Vadim yelled. 'And what a joy for Fyodor,' Kapa continued. 'What a nice surprise for him when he gets back and finds he's got a poppy and cocoa coloured baby!'
'Don't, Kapa!'
'I didn't say anything. It's none of my business. You sinned, you gave birth, you have to answer for it.
There was a bunch of flowers on the table. Anfisa was surprised.
'Who are they from?
'The nervous case bought them. Not exactly practical, are they, like a baby's vest or bonnet. Flowers, really!'
The 'nervous case', that's what Kapa called Olga Ivanovna; she didn't like her although she wasn't above taking her money to do her cleaning. Anfisa thought you shouldn't use someone like that if you didn't like them.
Olga Ivanovna returned later that evening. She kissed Anfisa in silence and silently examined Vadim with her blue, staring, yellow-ringed eyes. Her face twitched.
'Thank you for the flowers, Olga Ivanovna.'
'Don't mention it, Anfisa Maximovna. I'm very fond of you.'
It made Anfisa so happy that someone was fond of her.
Only Panka Zykova didn't come in to see her. She was

pretending not to be interested.

* *

Vadim did indeed turn out to be a self-willed and difficult baby. He yelled all day and he yelled almost uninterruptedly through the night. It could be said that his mouth never closed. You put him down to sleep and he screamed, you picked him up in your arms and he screamed, you stood him up and he screamed, you fed him and he'd suck his fill and scream again. And how he did scream! He'd go all blue and get into such a rage! Anfisa took him to the clinic and they said he's quite healthy, we can't imagine why he screams so much.

'Don't spoil him, mother! Feed him and put him back in his cot. He'll cry and cry, then he'll go to sleep.'

But Anfisa could never do that. If he cried it meant something was hurting him and that must be her fault. And he couldn't tell her where it hurt, poor little soul.

Anfisa carried him, Anfisa rocked him – but nothing worked. He even refused a dummy and spat it out as though he'd been mortally offended. It was a disaster! She got into the habit of rocking him with his head down – in that position Vadim would sometimes quieten down and drop off to sleep for half an hour or so. She too might have had a sleep then, but she simply couldn't. She would just doze off while she was feeding him sometimes – when he sucked she'd sleep. Anfisa never let herself feed him in bed either, for fear of smothering him. She'd feed him on a chair instead, and rock herself to sleep on the chair.

'He only screams because he hasn't been christened,' said Kapa. 'His soul is begging for some holy water. Christen him and he'll be meek as a lamb. D'you want me to arrange it?'

'Maybe I should?' Anfisa thought sometimes when she was at her wits' end. But she'd banish the thought immediately as unworthy of her. Let him grow up like every other child, like an ordinary soviet person. Otherwise he'd suddenly discover he'd been christened when he joined the Komsomol, and he'd never live it down.

Panka Zykova wasn't especially interested in the baby, thank God. So as to avoid irritating her Anfisa often boiled her swaddling clothes not in the kitchen but on a primus stove in her own room, and dried them on the radiator. She didn't mind, she soon got used to it. It was all like a dream. But it wasn't a dream. She was so exhausted from lack of sleep that she staggered around like a drunkard. She'd fall asleep on her feet. She'd go into the kitchen, fall asleep washing the baby clothes and wake up with her head falling into the water.

And then it was time for her to go back to work. She'd already got through all her allowance and her milk was beginning to give out. Vadim grew angry, tore at her breast and bawled even more furiously than ever – but it was from hunger now, so it was more understandable. At the clinic they gave her various bottles for him – B-Rice and C-Rice and so on – but he wouldn't hear of it, he wanted the breast, and more of it too. Anfisa sold all her non-essentials, then some of her essentials, like her slippers and her felt boots, and kept only her most necessary clothes. She owed everyone money – Olga Ivanovna, Ada Efimovna, Kapa. Panka was the only one she hadn't asked for money, she hadn't yet sunk that low. She got through all their money – and once again she was penniless. Like it or not she'd have to go back to work.

Olga Ivanovna, good as her word, found places for her and Vadim at the House of the Child, her as a childminder and him as an inmate, although it was against the rules really as he wasn't an orphan. So off they went to work, Anfisa to mind children and Vadim to bawl. He bawled to waken the dead and the staff got an earful of him. Anfisa deliberately left him in another group and herself worked with the toddlers and crawlers so as not to have to hear him and become too distraught. But she could always hear him, even through the wall. He had the loudest voice in the building.

Anfisa worked as diligently with the crawlers as she did every job of work, but she was wracked with such pity for them – for her own child and for other people's children. She regarded them all as hers, her heart ached for them all, crying and complaining and unable to speak. She didn't dare take them in her arms though; it wasn't allowed and she never had time. Feeding, changing, bathing – there was simply no time to turn around. Sometimes Anfisa just couldn't resist it and would pick a baby up in her arms, despite the rules. It would nestle up to her with its soft cheek and snotty nose, and she'd feel so unbearably sorry for it.

In the evening after work Anfisa would bundle Vadim up in his smart blanket and take him home. It was a long journey, by tram and bus. Vadim always slept on the way home for some reason, but the moment he got home he'd start bawling with renewed vigour. Yet he began to sleep more peacefully now – sometimes he'd sleep for almost two hours without creating an uproar, and she was thankful for that.

Vadim was better dressed than the other children, in soft flanelette nightshirts and little lacey vests which she had made with her last kopecks; and Ada Efimovna made him a little rabbit-down cap. No one made such things for the orphans or gave them presents.

As spring approached Vadim started to grow up; he learnt to sit and play with toys, and he screamed less and began to see reason. That summer he moved to the crawlers' group. He was unusually beautiful – his eyes had changed from milky pale to black, his eyelashes were long and his cheeks were pink. He was the prettiest baby in the whole group. He'd sit with the others in their walking frames and amongst them he looked like a heavenly prince. He had eyes like stars, curly hair and two teeth shining in his mouth like sugar. And when Olga Ivanovna played the piano to the crawlers and sang them songs Vadim understood better than the rest – he was musical! He began standing up on his hind legs and walking a few steps, and it was a joy to see him in his little blue trousers and reigns, grasping the side of the frame with one hand and shifting from leg to leg as though dancing. No one else in the crawlers' group could dance like him! He was ahead of all the rest; he started saying 'Mama!' and 'More!' before the others and he had such sturdy little legs, like tree trunks – he'd be a good walker all right! He started sleeping more quietly too, thank God! He only demanded attention three or four times a night now, and that was nothing, quite bearable. So life was really quite pleasant.

But more important, the war was coming to an end. The cannons boomed out salutes for one town after another, and the whole sky would explode with rockets and more rockets, like flowers. Anfisa loved the salutes. One evening she woke up her little boy and took him out to the street. 'Look, a salute!' she said. He looked obediently, waved his hand at each volley, and his eyes shone with multicoloured stars.

So the war was over, yes it really was over! Anfisa and Olga Ivanovna spent the night of the eighth and ninth glued to the radio. And the radio went wild! Cheerful songs, marches and dances all night! Yet they wouldn't announce the victory and the waiting became quite unbearable. Then at last they announced it! No one in the flat could sleep, and they kept the door on to the staircase open all night so that anyone could come in. People just walked in, complete strangers came and said hello. The janitor brought some vodka and proposed a toast to the 'honoured female collective', and they all drank, even Olga Ivanovna. They didn't sleep after that either. Next morning, when Olga Ivanovna, Anfisa and

Vadim went to work, news of the victory was already thundering through the streets. The whole town – millions and millions of people – had poured outside and the streets were black with people, red with flags. The House of the Child too. The infants, all tightly bundled up in their dark padded jackets, lined up on the pavement waving flags and singing 'Who goes into the forest for firewood . . .' And dinner was just like in peace time – Eulampia laid on a great spread, bringing all the food out of the cupboard and putting it on the table. They had chocolates and sweets too. Many of the babies had never seen a sweet before and didn't know how to unwrap them.

That evening after work Anfisa said: 'Olga Ivanovna, as you're here, would you mind keeping an eye on Vadim while I run out for a while?'

'Off you go, Anfisa Maximovna.'

Anfisa ran off where everyone else was running – to Red Square. People poured into it like water at flood tide. They kissed and embraced, officers and soldiers were thrown into the air, music and more music, the loudspeakers went wild, there were accordions at every street corner, everyone danced . . . A little soldier boy dragged Anfisa off to dance too, and she danced, quite forgetting her age. Danced and cried. All around her people were crying. And high above the square fluttered the red flag, like a fiery tongue . . .

Anfisa returned home, barely able to lift her feet. 'Well how was it?' asked Olga Ivanovna, her cheek twitching.

'Everyone danced and sang and cried, and so did I, fit to bring the house down,' she said.

Kapa came in from vespers. She brought some communion bread and told them the priest had proclaimed that it was for victory of the Russian army. Panka Zykova baked them all a cake . . .

So the war was over. A time of great happiness, but great sadness too. Many had lost their menfolk, people sobbed and wept, or drowned their sorrows. Anfisa rejoiced and waited and wept and feared lest Fyodor return. All the dates passed and still he didn't appear. So now she too must be a soldier's widow.

What could she do? She lived alone with her darling Vadim. Olga Ivanovna loved the little boy too and spoilt him terribly, bringing him toys and apples and little books which she would read to him. She gave him special attention at the House of the Child too, and cultivated his musical ear. He was gifted, she said. The others in the flat also liked Vadim for his good looks. Ada Efimovna would pet him every so often and so would Kapa, despite the fact he wasn't christened. Panka though, severe as ever, would just sail past him. She had become even more bad-tempered lately and there was good reason for it too, for she'd just been abandoned by her unregistered peasant. Just picked up his things one day and vanished into thin air. He hadn't lived with her very long, just long enough to grow bald. That always happened to women – he left her and went back home to someone else. The others would get together in the kitchen and discuss Panka's affairs. Kapa argued that it was right of him to go: a businesslike peasant doesn't sit around on his backside. Ada Efimovna, on the contrary, pitied Panka and condemned men as a class. One couldn't feel too sorry for Panka though: her face was black as an aspen trunk and she wouldn't confide in anyone. She wasn't a woman, she was a combine harvester.

[10]

I don't remember when and how it first occurred to me to compose music for children. I had never studied composition and never thought I'd be any good at it, but I tried and I was quite successful.

One evening we were sitting in the concert hall of the House of the Child – Anfisa was on cleaning duty and I had stayed behind to play the piano. Shyly at first and very quietly I started playing something of my own. Anfisa paid no attention.

'Anfisa Maximovna,' I said with beating heart. 'What d'you think of that?'

'It's all right,' said Anfisa absent-mindedly. 'Why?'

'I made it up.'

'You didn't!'

Anfisa's grey eyes opened so wide that I burst out laughing. 'What's so extraordinary about that? I made it up, that's all.'

But Anfisa couldn't believe her ears. 'Well, I never! A person making up music, just like that! What d'you call a person who makes up music then?'

'A composer.'

'So you're a composer?'

'No, of course not, nothing of the kind!'

'Well, if you composed it that means you're a composer.'

'You funny thing! There are all sorts of composers, great and small, and I'm the smallest minor composer there ever was. It's not even worth mentioning.'

Anfisa merely waved her hand: 'Small indeed! Why, you could give me a hundred thousand rubles but I couldn't compose something just like that!'

From then on Anfisa's respect for me grew beyond all bounds. I begged her not to tell anyone and she piously kept our secret, but she was bursting to tell. Sometimes I would play and she would lean over me and ask in a whisper: 'Did you compose that too?'

'No really, Anfisa Maximovna! That's Tchaikovsky!'

'Ah, I thought it was you.'

Once I composed a triumphal flourish for the children,

for dancing round the Christmas tree. I did it in the style of a polonaise, with a falling beat in every bar, and they would fall too. And how seriously they did it, all hobbling round and beaming with enthusiasm. It gave me quite a lump in my throat. 'Clap for Aunty Olga Ivanovna,' cried Anfisa (she knew the flourish was my own composition) and the children clapped their weak, damp little hands with a sound resembling the pattering of rain . . . Then I found some humorous verses in a magazine about a squirrel and a hedgehog and I set them to music. I can't think why, but the song was a great success and the children sang it with enthusiasm. From then on I was stricken with a positive mania for composing. I no longer stared out of the window when I couldn't sleep at nights, I composed music, humming it under my breath and accompanying myself on the blanket. At that time I even wanted (strangely enough!) to have my own piano . . . I had no real gift for composition of course, just a love of music and a good ear. Many well-read people can write fluently in the style of other people. I was like that. Nonetheless, at the time I was completely carried away by it. And I was encouraged by Anfisa's simple enthusiasm. She'd discovered a real expert!

Joking aside, the joy of creation, however unoriginal, warmed my soul. And when the children sang my songs it gave me so much more pleasure than when they sang other people's.

The most talented in the top class was Vadim Gromov. Handsome, bold, quick-witted, he sang better than the others, danced better than the others and said his 's's better than the others, hissing them with exceptional expertise. He was agile and active, always the ringleader in all the games, and able to recite a great many poems. Whenever some commission came to inspect us Eulampia Zakharovna always showed Vadim off: look what wonderful children we raise here, she'd say. He was indeed charming with his radiant dark good looks, his bright eyes and his quick legs.

It was only his haughtiness that disturbed me. He was a little king with his subjects. They'd seen nothing, he'd seen everything. They knew nothing, he knew everything.

'Stupid!' he'd say, showing off his 's'. 'Stupid boy hasn't seen a bus! I've been on a bus, and I've been on a tram!'

The children would listen to him as though he were a priest. He was the most experienced, the most beautiful, the most developed, the most . . .

* *

Then a great grief befell the House of the Child: our directress, Eulampia Zakharovna died. She died of stomach cancer, quickly and efficiently, as though knowing that she had cancer, that she had no hope, and that this was really quite an everyday occurrence. She went on working up to the very last weeks, overcoming her pain and weakness, making telephone calls and getting angry with people as usual. But then one day she grew terribly pale and closed her eyes as though unable to look her own death in the face. Ever since she'd fallen ill she'd been eager to talk to me about it and would often call me into her office without any special reason. I was apparently the only one amongst us who didn't lie to her or try to reassure her that she'd get better, and for this reason she valued me especially. We would have brief and businesslike talks together; death wasn't the main theme of our discussions, but it was always there. Eulampia Zakharovna would mention it in passing, in an offhand manner, not avoiding it but not dwelling on it either. There was some mention of the kitchen-garden, for instance. 'You'll be able to plant that out when I go,' she said calmly, and I didn't raise any objection as the conversation was a serious and businesslike one.

Once she asked me: 'Are you afraid of death Olga

Ivanovna?'

'No, I'm not afraid. I've died once already and I wasn't afraid then. But I love life and don't want to die.'

'I'm the same. I'm not afraid of death but I love life. If only I had just two more years, but it's not like that. I've only got three more months.'

'Nobody can know that . . . Maybe you'll live longer . . .'.

She looked at me patronisingly, as if I were a child: 'What are you talking about! And I thought you were a serious person!'

When Eulampia Zakharovna eventually took to her bed she was taken off to the hospital. I went there to visit her, and was amazed by the speed with which the illness had done its work. It was a skeleton I saw before me.

'What are you staring at?' she asked in a resonant voice, strangely out of keeping with the skeleton in the bed.

I didn't answer.

'Thank you for not lying to me. Everyone else lies. But you don't.'

What could I say? In these cases women usually cry, but I had no tears.

'Listen Olga Ivanovna, I'll tell you what dying is like. It's not a bit frightening. It seems like something very serious and difficult, and you don't know if you're going to have the strength for it. But then if you think about it a while, what strength d'you need to die? Death will do it all for you – she'll come and take you and soothe you while you lie there in your bed . . . And another thing, Olga Ivanovna, I keep wondering what the last moment will be like, and I think it'll be like vomiting, like vomiting my soul away.'

'Eulampia Zakharovna,' I said, taking her hand in mine, 'there's no death, you won't even feel it. Some philosopher said: "don't fear death – when you're alive it doesn't exist, and when you're dead it doesn't exist."'

'Very clever,' she observed, throwing me a sardonic

glance from her sunken eye sockets. 'Which philosopher was that then?'

'I don't remember.'

'Well, tell him he's lying.'

Eulampia Zakharovna closed her eyes. I left quietly.

A week later she was dead. The funeral was surprisingly well attended. We couldn't imagine who many of the people were: some soldiers, a priest with long hair pinned up under his soft cap, a brood of charming young girls who must have been sisters. Many of them wept; Nyura wept more than the rest, shrieking that it was because of the dead woman that she hadn't gone to the front, and now to punish her the war was over and her life was in ruins . . .

We buried her, wept for her and mourned her, and life resumed its normal course again, only without the directress. She was temporarily replaced by her elder sister, Yulia Ivanovna, an elderly trembling woman terrified of any sort of leadership or responsibility. She ran the House of the Child simply by not making any decisions, and keeping everything as it was before. So everything went on as it had done and the old established ways continued. I played my songs to the children and told them stories about Aunty Lanya, as they called Eulampia Zakharovna. In these stories Aunty Lanya was the good fairy. There was Cinderella too, in her tight shoes, and Cinderella was the very image of Anfisa Maximovna.

But one bad day they sent us a new directress from the city Health Department, a certain Inna Petrovna. She was a plump, fairly young woman, with masses of bright gold dyed hair piled on top of her proudly tossed-back head.

The moment she entered the House of the Child she said: 'What chaos! This is disgraceful!' and everyone fell silent. She set her lips as though squeezing them with pincers, and we realised that things were going to be hard. They certainly were too.

Inna Petrovna was unintelligent, spiteful and very full of herself as a pedagogue. What a terrible science that is! It uses the most dead words to evoke the most living things!

She paid no attention to me at first – there were more important things to set to rights first. She frightened Yulia Ivanovna out of her wits by intimating that she might be arrested for dereliction of duty, and Yulia Ivanovna tried to justify herself by saying that was how things had always been done under the late Eulampia Zakharovna.

'It's all too easy to blame the dead,' said our new directress, pinching her lips.

She spoke like this so often to Nyura that eventually the poor girl couldn't take any more and handed in her notice.

'We shan't weep for her,' said Inna Petrovna. 'No one is irreplaceable. But her reference is in our hands.'

And when she gave Nyura her reference it couldn't have been worse – individualism, indiscipline, anarcho-syndicalist temperament . . . Nyura threw the reference on the floor and spat: 'Does she think I'm sunk without a reference? Thank God I work with my hands, not my head.'

It took Inna Petrovna about three months to get round to me. She started by asking me where I got my teaching material. Some of it was songs, I said. Who had authorised them? she asked. I had to confess that no one had authorised my little songs. The directress was horrified and started clucking like a hen; 'What's this, what's this?'

After she had calmed down a little she explained that I had committed a grave breach of discipline; the use of unapproved and unchecked teaching material at this time was tantamount to idealogical diversion. In one nursery school they had even sung pre-revolutionary songs! The directress had been dismissed, of course. One must always remember that children aren't merely singing – they're shaping their world view in the process . . .

Both children and songs withered and died under her words. 'Do you understand?'

'I understand.'

She was silent for a while, sensing some sort of dirty trick. 'You can treat me as you want, I merely demand that discipline is maintained. I trust there will be no more infringements.'

'There won't,' I assured her.

And there weren't. My activities as a composer came to an end. For some time afterwards, especially at night, I was haunted by absurd sounds, the light syncopes of polkas – but it passed. No one could actually forbid me to compose though, no one could check each note to see whether I was playing my own piece or someone else's. The main thing was to kill the desire, and this Inna Petrovna had managed to do. But I and my music didn't matter. What did matter was that Anfisa, the most loving and talented of all the childminders, was eventually forced to leave. Love is a rare talent, and Anfisa possessed it in generous measure. But Inna Petrovna, as is often the way with professional leaders, had an unerring nose for anything fresh and original. She would immediately drag it out into the light and destroy it. That's what happened to Anfisa.

[11]

Vadim had grown pretty big. He was four by now, and too old for the House of the Child. That was true, of course. But he wasn't an inmate, he was a special case –

his mother brought him there just for the day, and took him home to sleep; he was bigger, more developed and better fed than the others because Anfisa devoted her entire life to him. She herself now worked as a teacher in the oldest group, the three-year-olds, and Vadim too was in that group. 'The two of us together,' Anfisa would console herself. 'That's how it'll always be. Him in the creche and me in the creche, him in the school and me in the school. And when he goes to the Institute I'll go to the Institute too. Maybe they'll give me a job as a cleaner there. Cleaners are in short supply these days!'

The late Eulampia Zakharovna had never raised any objection to Vadim being there. Where was one supposed to put a child whose mother worked? No, let her bring him.

Anfisa didn't love just her own child, she loved all the children. No one could ever accuse her of singling out her own, ask who you like. But in the older group she did have her favourites. She especially loved the curly-haired ones. Once in a while she'd even kiss them. In Eulampia Zakharovna's day this was perfectly all right: kiss whoever you want, do whatever you want just so long as you don't hit them. But the new directress was adamantly against it.

'Anfisa Maximovna, it is forbidden to kiss individual children!'

Individual children indeed! Do they have to be kissed collectively then? But she didn't say anything and didn't argue. She knew she hadn't had much education – just six classes, and that nursing course during the war – and the others had all had a university education. They could sack you without a university education too, and that terrified Anfisa: she was used to being there with her son by now. So she tried to broaden her education and catch up on her reading. She joined a library and they gave her some little books on pre-school teaching methods. She read and she read and she couldn't make head nor tail of any of it. They wrote a lot, but it was all so pointless. They talked about the peculiarities of age psychology, and about the child's personality as tediously as if they were rinsing an old bag. But what did they mean by personality? All that mattered was the child: love him and play with him – and he'll love you back.

The children did indeed love Anfisa and always turned to her with their questions. For instance: 'Anfisa Maximovna, what's a goose for?' (The children had never seen a goose as they'd grown up in the city.) So Anfisa would explain as best she could: 'The goose has feathers, feathers give us pillows and pillows give us sweet downy dreams. Sleep tight little baby, says the dream. And the little baby sleeps and silver bells ring in her ears . . .'

'Bells . . .' repeated the children. Then another would ask: 'Why is the goose better than the hen?'

And she would have an answer ready for that too: 'Because the goose has a neck. It can see far with that neck, to the very edge of the world. The man at the edge of the world asks: "Who's looking at me from such a great height?" And they say: "Why it's a goose!"' And the children would be happy.

They'd come straight to her when they got into fights. 'He hit me, Anfisa Maximovna!'

'And what did you do?'

'I hit him back!'

'So you're both all right then,' Anfisa would say. 'Now both of you come here, one in my right arm and one in my left. I've got two hands here, two little houses, and in each house there's a stove, and in each house there's a candle, and in each house there's a pennyweight and a pepper-box . . .'

The children loved this and would begin to play house. But the directress heard. 'What's all this about pennyweights and pepper-boxes?' she said. 'Where did that come from? A pennyweight is a pre-revolutionary unit of measurement and we no longer have pepper-boxes.'

'Anfisa Maximovna told us,' they said.

Inna Petrovna twisted her lip in a grimace. Then: 'Anfisa Maximovna, the children have been quoting you.'

'What d'you mean?' asked Anfisa, startled.

'About a pennyweight and a pepper-box . . . '

'Oh that! It's just some nonsense I told them and then forgot about.'

'Nonsense has no place in the education of children. The educator must promote with every word, every step . . .'

'You fool, you stupid over-educated fool,' thought Anfisa wearily. 'I wish I'd had your schooling.'

One day a little fish died.

'Thoughts about an animal's death should not shadow the happy childhood of a soviet child,' Anfisa said to herself in the directress's voice as the tears flowed. Not just for the fish but for herself, for Fyodor, for Vadim, for all the little orphans . . .

Soon the directress got to Vadim. She started cavilling at the fact that he was too old, that his mother was breaking the rules by taking him home every evening, and thus encouraging germs to spread. And she demanded that Vadim be removed from the House of the Child and moved to an ordinary nursery school in the town.

Anfisa Maximovna fretted and held her tongue. She really didn't want to leave. But the directress went on plaguing her like an autumn fly: 'If a government commission discovered such an infringement they'd be entitled to dismiss me from my job.'

It was the last straw. Goodbye House of the Child. Anfisa went there for the last time, wept, kissed everyone and said goodbye, while Vadim stood to one side, hanging his head and angrily kicking the ground with his heel. What was he thinking?

The following day Anfisa and Vadim would be going off to a new kindergarten in the town. How would it be there? 'It doesn't matter,' thought Anfisa. 'The main thing is we'll be together, where you go I go too.'

* *

The new kindergarten turned out to be large and spacious, and far better appointed than the House of the Child. It was the last word in modernity. In the w.c.'s they had not chamberpots but special low children's lavatories like little toadstools. There were new little cupboards and clothes-dryers too, and the children slept outside on the verandah in sleeping bags. And the playground had everything you could possibly imagine, including swings and roundabouts! The children there were robust and well-fed – they were mainly the children of scientists, who had the best rations as they were allocated to the best distributors. Anfisa was hired as a teacher in the middle group – they considered that her experience compensated for her lack of education – and Vadim went into the infants' class. Well, no matter – it wasn't such a big separation, she was on the first floor and he was on the second.

At first Anfisa fretted and missed the House of the Child and her curly-haired little pets. Here the children were livelier and better developed, which meant that they were more self-centered too. And they had terrible fights. But she gradually got used to it, and the children grew to love her. You had to be able to look after intellectuals' children too, after all. The new directress was all right, although she was rather a tiresome person who sounded as though she was crying when she spoke.

But Vadim didn't take at all kindly to the place. He simply couldn't get used to the idea that he wasn't the most important person there. In the mornings he'd whimper: 'I don't want to go to the nursery, I want to go to the little house!' (That's what he called the House of the Child.) Anfisa found this very touching. 'He's so faithful to his little house! He won't betray his wife when he gets married!'

But Vadim just missed his accustomed worship. He didn't get it at the nursery, and he didn't like that at all. Once he went up to his teacher in the infants' class and touched her elbow, saying: 'Hey look, it's me!'

She looked at him calmly and cheerfully with her round black eyes. 'Why should I look at you?'

'It's me, it's me!'

'Well I never! It's the Moscow Arts Theatre in person!' She wasn't at all impressed by him, and Vadim found this utterly mortifying. And he was unable to express what he was missing too.

Eventually he settled down at the new nursery, but he never really liked it.

[12]

Vadim was four when Fyodor unexpectedly returned.

It was in the evening; Anfisa had bathed her son, put him to bed, gone to the shop and returned home – and there was Fyodor, sitting on a chair by the cot, looking silently at the child. Anfisa was stunned. Her arms and legs went numb and her heart pounded.

'Hello Anfisa,' said Fyodor without getting up.

'Hello Fedya,' Anfisa replied almost inaudibly.

'So this is what you've been up to,' he said.

'You must stay here,' said Anfisa hurriedly. 'It's your home, you live here and we'll leave.'

'Why should you two leave? It's better if I leave. I'm the man.'

He stood up, straightened his shoulders and walked

about the room. Then she noticed that one of his legs was shorter than the other. She burst into tears of pity.

'Tut tut,' said Fyodor, 'don't start snivelling. It's miserable enough without that. Is there any vodka?'

'No, there isn't, Fedya. I'll ask Kapa. Maybe she has some.'

'Go on then.'

Anfisa went to Kapa and sure enough she had a bottle. Resourceful woman, she had everything. 'Take it,' she said, 'it's a special occasion.' And added: 'Fyodor must be pleased. Has he beaten you yet?'

'No not yet.'

'What's he going to do then?'

'He hasn't said anything. He's just looking at Vadik.* Oh, I'm terrified Kapa, what'll happen?'

'There there, you've got yourself into trouble, now you must answer for it. That's what you get for gadding around . . .'

Anfisa took the vodka, put it on the table with some black bread, onion and dried fish, poured him a glass and covered her knees with a towel. Fyodor sat down. 'Why only one glass? Pour one for yourself.'

'I don't drink, Fedya.'

'Have a drink just this once, then.'

They filled their glasses and emptied them in silence.

'Well then,' said Fyodor.

'It just happened, it's all my fault, I don't know how it happened . . .'

'I don't blame you for anything. There's nothing more to say about it . . .'

He pointed his chin at the cot where the baby slept, his arms above his head, looking extraordinarily beautiful with his long eyelashes.

'Boy?'

'Yes, a little boy.'

* *Affectionate diminutive for Vadim.*

'What's his name?'

'Vadim.'

'Patronymic?'

Anfisa looked confused. Fyodor grinned on one side of his face and said: 'Well, he can be Fyodorovich if that's all right by you!'

'Fedenka!' Anfisa threw herself at Fyodor's feet. Forgetting herself, she embraced his knees in their worn cotton breeches, cried out and apologised. Fyodor fastidiously freed his legs from her embrace and pushed her wet face away from his knees. 'That's enough Fisa, don't yell. It's not the cinema. I said it, and that's an end to it. Get up and sit down at the table to celebrate.'

Anfisa sat down limply on the edge of her chair.

'Drink!'

'I'm not used to it . . .'

'Well I am!'

Fyodor drank glass after glass, got drunk and gloomy and shook with grief. Then he told her to bring his guitar. (It was a good thing she hadn't sold it!) The strap was all crumpled and Fyodor tore it off in a rage and threw it on the floor. Then he tried the strings. One was missing, the others were hopelessly out of tune. He threw the guitar on the bed, she sobbed and Fyodor started singing without his guitar, howling in a wild voice something about the fire of Moscow. He got up, staggered, clenched his fists (Anfisa lowered her head and hunched her shoulders), and asked: 'Are you afraid?' then burst out laughing. He fell on to his knees, with his head on the chair – which crashed to the ground. Was he going to sleep? No, he was silent. Anfisa held her breath and listened: not a sound from him. Soon there was a weak childish snore. He must be asleep, thank the Lord.

Anfisa dragged the senseless Fyodor, heavy as lead, to her bed, took off his boots, unbuttoned his field shirt and covered him with a blanket. Then she lay down on the floor.

Next morning she got up quietly so as not to disturb him, woke up the little boy and dressed and fed him. Vadim goggled at his strange uncle with sleepy eyes and whimpered as usual: 'I don't want to go to the nursery, I want to go to the little house!'

'Hush my pet,' whispered Anfisa. 'We'll see the rabbit and the tortoise. The rabbit's had a nice sleep and is going knock, knock, knock with his little legs. "Where are you, tortoise?" he says. "I've missed you . . ."'

They went off, and when they returned Fyodor was drunk for the next four days too, without waking up. He didn't shout, he didn't make an uproar, he would just crash to the ground, stricken, and would sink into oblivion.

'Lord, he's epileptic,' thought Anfisa. 'And it's all my fault.'

On the fifth day Fyodor came to his senses and said: 'That's it, I've finished celebrating now. Time to start living.'

So they started living. Fyodor wasn't in any hurry to find work, he had money – although where it came from Anfisa had no idea, and she didn't ask either. 'It's none of my business,' she thought. ' A man's his own master.' She didn't know whether he received a pension either, although as an invalid he must do. Fyodor would give her the housekeeping money, simply putting it down on the table in silence. He never said how long it was supposed to last, and she just had to work it out as best she could.

During the day, while Anfisa and Vadim were at the nursery, Fyodor would sit at home making cigarette lighters and cases out of plexiglass (most likely to sell, since they would invariably disappear). Again, Anfisa wouldn't interfere. He developed a rasping cough, and he never smiled now. He did play with the little boy though. He loved the child and called him Vadim Fyodorovich. Anfisa, always conscious of the wrong she'd done him, was shy and deferential with him. In the mornings she'd lay the table for breakfast: 'D'you want to eat, Fyodor?'

'Leave it, I'll get my own.'

He always got his own, as though someone was trying to poison him.

He didn't drink every day, but every two or three months he'd have a binge. He didn't shout or create an uproar – he would simply collapse. Once he beat Anfisa. He'd been drinking heavily and there was no more money left. 'Give me some and I'll write you a cheque,' he said.

'I don't have any, Fedya,' she said, and that was the truth. Then he beat her. He cut her lip and made it bleed, then he went out. When he came back he was sober.

'Forgive me Fisa, I don't know what's happening to me. I must get a job.'

Anfisa started crying too, of course.

'But it's my fault . . . It's all right if you hit me Fedenka. It's better than I deserve.' Fyodor waved her aside disdainfully.

He soon did get a job – at a repair workshop. Although he was an invalid he still had the use of his hands and didn't break the instruments.

[13]

After Fyodor Gromov returned our flat changed. The atmosphere became slightly more formal – we had a man in the house now, after all; a lawful head of household. The women no longer went about looking like slovens in their shabby dressing-gowns. Something sweet and almost virginal would flit over their faces when they made way for him in the corridor, trying to appear younger, smaller and more elegant . . . My God, I thought, how terrible and pathetic, and how human.

There were fewer arguments too – people were embarrassed to quarrel in front of Fyodor.

But Fyodor, strange as it may seem, made friends with me. He visited me first at my request, to mend my radio. He mended it and brought it back, then stood there looking at the books. Then he started up a conversation. He visited me regularly after that. Every so often he'd knock at the door: 'Olga Ivanovna, are you busy?'

'No, of course not, come in, Fyodor Savelevich.'

He would come in, sit down sideways on the chair so as to take up less space (I would sit on the bed – maybe I should have brought in another chair?), and launch into a conversation: 'Olga Ivanovna, is it true what they say, that in America they've invented a machine that solves problems on its own, without people?'

'I don't know, Fyodor Savelevich, it may well be true.'

'And what d'you think about it? D'you think it's a good thing or not? The newspapers say it's bad; idealism they call it.'

'I don't think there's anything bad about it. I could never solve problems when I was at school, and I never learnt afterwards either. But I'd have been able to do them if they'd given me one of those machines. What's so bad about that?'

Fyodor laughed. He had a strange laugh, like a cough. But his eyes were kind and blue.

He kept asking me things. He thought I was educated. But I'm really very ignorant. I often regret that I'm so ignorant. To most of his questions I had to reply 'I don't know'.

'What d'you think Olga Ivanovna, did Hitler really commit suicide? Apparently it's all lies – they found some sort of dummy there instead of Hitler.'

'I don't know, Fyodor Savelevich.'

'If they brought Hitler to you and said: "Kill him if you want," would you kill him?'

'I don't know . . . No, I don't think I would.'

'Nor would I. I wouldn't kill anyone.'

'But you've fought in the war. Didn't you have to kill then?'

'I never saw the faces of the people I killed, though. I wouldn't have been able to do it if I had. I think everyone's the same. Show someone the face of the person he has to kill and he gets scared and can't do it . . . It's a hard problem . . .'

Sometimes he would ask me about myself: 'Now you had a university education. What did they teach you there?' he asked once.

'Music.'

'I didn't think music was something you studied. We did music in our amateur talent club – I thought it was like that, something you did just for pleasure.'

'But there are amateurs and professionals in everything, Fyodor Savelevich. I open a tin as an amateur, for instance, while you do it as a professional.'

He laughed. Then: 'So what's your profession?'

'Pianist.'

'Why don't you have a piano then?'

'I did. It's a long story. It was destroyed with my house when the bomb fell . . .'

His brow darkened and he was silent a moment. Then with an effort he said: 'I'm sorry Olga Ivanovna, I shouldn't have asked. I won't ask any more if you don't want me to.'

'No please do, I don't mind at all.'

'I just wanted to know . . . You lost everything, and you're still alive – where d'you get the strength from? If it's hard for you, don't answer.'

'No I'll try. Life is always a struggle. You've seen grass forcing its way through asphalt?'

'Yes.'

'A little blade of grass, but it has such strength . . .'
'I understand.'
Or some really strange questions: 'D'you think a cow feels anything?'
'I don't really know, I should think it feels *something*.'
'When they take her calf away and slaughter it, for instance, does she grieve?'
'Certainly she grieves. But in her own way, not like us.'
'Well, I think she grieves like us. It's just that we can't see her grief. In the cow it's more deeply buried.'
A strange person, but a good one. He would sit with me for a while, then leave.
'Forgive me, Olga Ivanovna. I'm taking up so much of your time with all this talk?'
'What are you talking about, Fyodor Savelevich? I'm delighted to see you.'
We got quite used to one another, and I even started to ask him some questions. Like 'Why do you drink, Fyodor Savelevich?'
'I don't know myself why I do it. There's nothing to be said for it, but still I do it. You're sobbing inside with depression sometimes, and there's nothing you can do but drink. And then it doesn't matter any more and everything seems better.'
'But you should think of poor Anfisa Maximovna.'
'I do think of her, all the time. That's why I drink.'
He generally avoided talking about Anfisa, yet he seemed eager to do so too – he both avoided and longed for it. Once he said grudgingly, curling his lip: 'What does she want? She thinks she's wronged me, and it makes her so obliging and eager to please. But I find it even more unbearable when she's like that.' He paused, then added: 'She suffocates me.'
He spoke enthusiastically about the boy though, always calling him 'my son and heir Vadim Fyodorovich'. It was evident from his eyes and smile that Vadim was very dear to him and that he was proud of his beauty and his

cleverness. Once he said: 'You may laugh, but I love that other man's son like my own. I've forgotten he isn't mine, believe it or not.'

'I certainly do believe it.'

'Could you love another person's child like your own?'

'I certainly could.'

Of course Fyodor's visits didn't pass unnoticed in the flat, and the other women – apart from Anfisa – were all amicably jealous of me. A strange sort of jealousy, without love or any real foundation. A poor surrogate emotion, occurring where life hadn't been fully lived and love hadn't been fully loved: none of the women in our flat had had their fill of life, love or jealousy.

It cost me something to go to the kitchen, where I would be submerged by their envy. Panka Zykova's sidelong glance as she dashed past with an iron in her hand, Kapa's malicious smile, and the sullen glance out of her round little eye, even Ada, bustling around frantically – it all spelt one thing: jealousy!

Curious . . . I with my walking-stick, an object of jealousy? It was absurd!

Only Anfisa wasn't jealous. On the contrary, she was pleased. Thank God Fyodor at last had someone to whom he could unburden his heart.

'Olga Ivanovna, it's so good that you have some influence over him. Maybe you could cure him of his drinking? That would be marvellous! He has such respect for you . . .'

'I'll try, Anfisa Maximovna, but I doubt it.'

'Please try though. And I'll wash the floors for you and do anything you want!' There was hope in her eye. But then things changed . . .

Kapa, like a good neighbour, tried to tell Anfisa that she should keep a closer watch on that little husband of hers. But Anfisa sent her packing good and proper. She told me all about it. ' "Don't you dare!" I shouted at her. "She and Fyodor have a pure friendship! Don't you dare talk like that about her with your dirty tongue!" That's what I said, and I was shaking like the palsy. I really lost my temper with her. She was terrified and shot out of the kitchen like a cat who's been naughty and runs off before they can stick his nose in it. I threw a fork after her. And I didn't hear a squeak out of her for the rest of the evening!'

[14]

Then Ada Efimovna came in to see me. She sat on the bed, decorously crossing her little feet, her arched insteps like two onions, and said decisively: 'Now then, we must talk. I'm getting tired of these Athenian nights.'

'What nights?'

'Athenian nights – you know, mysteries and jealousy and the rest of it. You know what I mean – Fyodor Savelevich. I've finally decided to let you have him.'

'What d'you mean, let me have him?'

'Don't interrupt, let me finish. I've worked it all out very neatly, and this is how it is. He clearly doesn't love his wife. So he now has a choice – you or me. At first I thought I'd have him myself. Of course he has his faults, although one can't really quibble over his lack of manliness. But I thought it all over and I came to the conclusion that I wouldn't find happiness there. In the first place, I can't bear the smell of vodka. Of course it might be possible to reform him, but I have such a weak feminine character – I'm just not the right person to do it. So who is? You are, of course! So I summoned up all my magnanimity and came to see you. Take him, reform him, he's yours. He'll marry you, you'll re-educate him and he'll make you a splendid husband. Anfisa will be grateful to you for saving him and she'll be happy too. And everything will be for the best and everthing will be wonderful.'

I listened to her, stupefied, unable to find anything to say. It was completely idiotic and incomprehensible.

'So shall we shake hands on it?' asked Ada, and laughed her resonant laugh. Whenever I hear this laugh I always turned round to look for a man.

'This is quite mad,' I said. 'It's ridiculous. Nothing of the sort has entered my head, I assure you. Or his, for that matter.'

'But what about his love for you?' slyly asked Ada.

'What love? There's no love between us and there never could be!'

Ada wagged her finger menacingly at me. 'Who do you think you're fooling? Not me! He's madly in love with you, like a troubadour. Or Tristan, I don't remember which.'

I shrugged my shoulders and stood up. 'Ada Efimovna, stop making up stories. Now please, let's not talk about it any more, all right?'

She looked disappointed but resigned, and went out.

How ridiculous! I'd just have to try and forget about it.

But when Fyodor next came in to see me there was something between us. I watched him more attentively than before. Tristan. Troubadour. Could Ada have been right? She couldn't be. Nonsense. A figment of her fevered fantasy life. Yet all the same . . .

Every time he came to see me it became more and more obvious: it was ridiculous, but Ada was right. Fyodor was in love with me. The special voice he used, the way he stood in the doorway, the melting looks from his bloodshot blue eyes . . . Once he brought me a bunch of flowers in a milk bottle. He clicked his heels as he proudly and shyly put them on the table, and I was no longer in any doubt: he was in love with me. Or perhaps even worse, he loved me. Yes, he loved me.

This thought was terrible because of Anfisa. But I wasn't only worried about her. Well, all right, so Fyodor loved me, but what about me? Of course not, I couldn't love anyone, least of all Fyodor. Why then did the thought of his love make me so happy? Could it be that like the others, I hadn't lived or loved enough? Could it be that in me too there lived a woman begging for charity? That I, this freakish creature without sex or age, with my lameness and my stick, was still a woman who needed to be loved?

When I went to work the next morning the birds sang, my stick seemed light and I smiled at the knowledge that I was loved. I even smiled at the directress, who was looking unhappy that day. I was overjoyed to see the children and boldly sang them a forbidden song. I was happy for several days . . .

Then everything started to go wrong. From Anfisa's face I realised that she knew. Anfisa had a rare shrewdness and sensitivity. One morning I saw her angry face . . . And I knew what I had to do: I had to break it off at once. It was absurd, nothing had happened, but what hadn't happened had to be broken off.

When Fyodor came in to see me with yet another bunch of flowers I said to him: 'Fyodor Savelevich, you mustn't come here any more.'

He paled and understood everything. 'Did she tell you to say that?'

'No, I did.'

Fyodor said nothing, then said: 'Pah!', hit his thigh with the flowers and limped out of the room. I looked at his back and I remember I was struck by the fact that we were both crippled; I'd never noticed before that he was lame.

Fyodor didn't come in to see me any more after that. When he met me in the corridor he would merely nod his head at me in silence. I learnt from Kapa that he was drinking even more heavily than before. Once I went to the telephone and a voice said: 'Is Gromov yours? This is the sobering-up station. You can come and collect him.' Dying of shame, I called Anfisa to the telephone. Her face wore an expression of such implacable hostility towards me as she said: 'Yes, yes . . . ', and repeated the address.

Then Fyodor was given the sack for drunkenness and truancy. Thank God he wasn't sentenced: the director took pity on him as a front line soldier and saved him from that.

After losing his job Fyodor stayed at home. He sold his suit and his guitar, then he started asking Anfisa for money. She wouldn't give him any; he would swear at her and go off with his friends, returning in the most terrible state with his clothes all torn. I learnt all this from Kapa: Anfisa almost never spoke to me now. When Fyodor came out to the kitchen in the morning his hands would shake and his trousers hung loosely on his waist . . . He would turn away whenever he saw me. The women no longer cared about their appearance now. Ada Efimovna would come into the kitchen in her curlers, and at the sight of Fyodor she would toss her head and the curlers would jingle disapprovingly. But it wasn't Fyodor she disapproved of, it was me. And I suppose it was my fault in a way: a man had started visiting me, brought me flowers, and I, heartless idiot that I am, had driven him away . . . But what could I have done. Explain everything to Anfisa? What was there to explain anyway?

As far as I could see Fyodor had only one joy in his life now – Vadim. He had grown into a big, beautiful, agile boy, and he adored his father. To his mother he was almost indifferent, and calmly accepted her slavish devotion to him, but his father was constantly in his thoughts. It was always 'Papa said', or 'Papa did', or 'Look, Papa's coming . . .' They lived a wretchedly impoverished life; Anfisa wore herself out and looked aged and yellow.

It all had a terrible ending: Fyodor fell under a tram. He fell face-down straight on to the rails, and the driver hadn't time to brake. It was a Sunday, a bright, sunny autumn day. I remember the desperate cry on the stairs: 'Fiska, come quick, your husband's been run over by a tram!' I remember how we all dashed out with Anfisa, led to the spot by a dense, noisy crowd of people, who all seemed so animated and cheerful. I ran with my stick, limping and gasping. Anfisa howled and tore her hair. I remember how the crowd parted, and in the middle, lying on the rails, were some yellow maple leaves ('Caution. Falling Leaves!'), some blood and something pink, something strangled and horribly resembling a slaughtered calf. Fyodor himself I didn't see because I dropped down onto my knees beside Anfisa – she had fallen and struck her head on the asphalt, and I put out my hand to protect her head . . .

'It was because of me he was killed!' She screamed. 'It's all my fault! Arrest me, arrest me!'

We lifted her up and helped her home, and she kept shouting: 'Arrest me, arrest me!'

Only Vadim was at home when we got back. I found him cowering terrified in the kitchen, whimpering and shivering. He was about six now and he understood quite a bit, although he didn't want to understand, and protected himself from suffering, as children always do. I took him off to my room and he clung to me, listened to me and shivered: 'Who's that screaming?' It was Anfisa.

'No one's screaming any more,' I said. 'You're imagining it.' By then the screaming had stopped.

I showed Vadim some pictures, sang him a funny song and gave him a sweet, and soon he was laughing, looking at the pictures with chocolate all over his mouth and great tears on his trembling eyelashes. The flat was quiet now. The little boy laughed. Soon he grew tired and fell asleep on my bed.

I didn't let him out of my sight throughout the three

days before Fyodor's funeral. I took him off to the House of the Child with me, telling him that he was my assistant, and he entered into this role eagerly, wiping the infants' noses and scolding them when they wet their pants. The directress frowned at this infringement of the rules, but she didn't say anything.

She had a superstitious respect for death, like most vulgar people. I was haunted by the thought that she was unhappy, and that her pincer-like mouth was merely the outward resistance to her grief . . .

In the evenings Vadim would fall asleep on my bed and I would sleep beside him, afraid to turn on my squeaking radio and wake him up. That little boy was so dear to me . . .

I don't know what happened to Anfisa in those three days. I saw her only after the funeral, at the dinner. She had aged ten years; she didn't cry, just chewed her headscarf and twitched her head.

The next day I went in to see her. She was standing with her face to the window and her back to the door. She turned round when she heard my footsteps. I went up to her and we embraced. We leant against one another and I kissed her, moving a lock of stiff damp hair off her forehead with my lips.

[15]

After Fyodor's death it seemed quite natural somehow that Anfisa, Vadim and I should start living together as a family. The boy had grown attached to me and I had grown to love him; and Anfisa was like a sister to me.

Sometimes she and I quarrelled, for she had become

very nervous, almost hysterical at times, and I was no better – I was forever taking offence over trifles. I should have controlled my temper, for she was in a far worse state than I was. We quarrelled over the stupidest things imaginable.

Anfisa's housework, for instance. One day she washed the floor, tidied the kitchen, went off to the bath-house and had a good steam and returned home pink, happy and rejuvenated. She asked me if I wanted some tea. I was washing clothes in the kitchen. I hadn't watched what I was doing and had spilt some water on the floor. 'Hah, a real lady, I see!' said Anfisa, angrily, her flashing eyes looking especially grey against the pink of her cheeks. 'You just read your books all day, never mind us workers! I think I'll splash the floor today, the working class can clear it up!'

'Oh Lord, Anfisa Maximovna, me a lady? Why, I'm just as much of a worker as you are!'

'Yes, but you're not really much of one, are you! I do my housework and yours, while you have a nice little rest with a book.'

I couldn't stand for that and burst out: 'Aren't you ashamed of yourself! You know I have a bad back. If it's come to that I'll pay you to do my cleaning!'

Anfisa burst into tears and said: 'I shan't take another kopeck from you! You can beg, you can fall down on your knees, you can do anything you like! And don't give Vadim any more sweets either! Kapa's right about you – you're a nervous case! A stuck-up lady!'

I should have laughed, but instead I took offence and nursed my resentment. For several days we didn't speak. It was painful for her and it was painful for me. When Anfisa and I were quarrelling Kapa was happy: 'I warned you about that nervous case,' she'd say to Anfisa. 'Lord knows what goes on inside her head!'

Kapa liked it when we were quarrelling because then she could do my cleaning for me, and that meant a little extra money for her. Anfisa would angrily watch Kapa washing the kitchen floor and sink for me; in her opinion she did it badly. Communal rivalry would rage – over the floor, the sink, my kopecks. But Anfisa was utterly selfless, I knew that.

When we quarrelled I felt as though a window had been opened, letting in an icy draught. I knew I ought to go and apologise to her, but my pride wouldn't let me. So we both went on sulking, and when we passed one another in the corridor I could feel the weight of her hatred on my back.

We made it up slowly and with great difficulty. Anfisa baked some pies, silently dumped them on the table for me to try and went off.

'Anfisa Maximovna!' I shouted after her.

Anfisa Maximovna pursed her lips: 'I didn't do it for any particular reason, just to be neighbourly. Take them, I don't hold a grudge.'

'Well, I don't need them!'

'I said I didn't bear a grudge. It's you who begrudge the slightest bit of kindness.'

I picked up the pies, took them to the kitchen and put them on the table, cursing myself for my pettiness. Anfisa threw the pies in the rubbish bin, shaking all over: 'Ah, so you're too good for me, are you? Well, I've got my pride too! You just wait!'

A moment later my door burst open and one of my presents to her flew into the room. Over the years of living together quite a few presents had accumulated, so there was always something for her to throw. I was incensed too by then, and threw the present into the rubbish bin, whereupon Kapa fished it out, saying: 'Stupid women, spoiling good things! I'm not proud, I'll take it!' So Kapa triumphed and I went to my room, choking and furious with myself.

It was such a relief and a joy when we did eventually make it up.

I have a great failing: I can never take the first step. Even if I was dying, I just couldn't do it. Anfisa is a better person than me, more magnanimous. She would come into my room, her face so kind, her eyes shining, a dimple on her cheek. She was very beautiful at such moments.

'Forgive me, Olga Ivanovna, I've been very stupid.'

'Anfisa Maximovna my dear, *you* must forgive *me*.'

We would embrace and Anfisa would cry, but I couldn't. I would feel her trembling shoulder beneath my arm, she would raise her wet shining eyes to mine and we would both laugh. That's how our life was together.

Between us Vadim grew up to be a handsome, cheeky, spoilt child. We both vied with each other in spoiling him and were rivals for his love; it was a blessing we didn't have much money or we would have spoilt him completely. When we quarrelled Vadim would understand and cunningly take first one side then the other. Sometimes it seemed to me that he didn't really like either of us. But there you are – I loved him despite everything! How lovely he was when he got up to some mischief and came running to me to boast about it, his eyes shining: 'Aunty Olyanna, I've done something bad!'

Vadim grew, and it was soon time for him to go to school. Anfisa wept: 'We've never been separated before. When he went to the little house I went there too, when he went to the nursery I went too, and I thought when he went to school I'd go too. But how can I? What would I do there? Get a job as a childminder or a janitor? The pay would be almost nothing. As least I get fed at the nursery school.'

We talked it over and we finally decided that Anfisa should stay at the nursery when Vadim went to school. It was such a joy to give the little boy his satchel, his pencil-case and his ABC. He stood there all ready to go, looking so grown-up in his baggy little trousers, his satchel in his hand. We took him to the school, I kissed his downy cheek and he coolly turned away. Anfisa cried, of course. He loathed women's tears. He firmly walked through the door into the school.

So for the first time in their lives they were apart.

[16]

Vadim went to school, Anfisa to the nursery and I to the House of the Child, dragging myself out of bed every morning and frequently exhausted by the directress's eternal nagging. She became even more petty, spiteful and stubborn, as though taking her unhappiness out on others. There were rumours that her husband had left her for a young girl. One evening I found her sitting slumped in the hall, her head lolling over the back of her chair. That head looked like a large golden flower, broken by the wind. At the sound of my step she raised it and quickly snapped her face shut. But it was too late: I'd seen her human eyes.

In the House of the Child there was a spate of quarantines: measles, chickenpox, then whooping cough. The whooping cough cases weren't isolated properly and the children would burst out into prolonged coughing and be unable to sing.

Communal life in the flat resumed its normal course. Passions flared continually for various reasons, mainly petty ones. I had long ago learnt not to despise the pettiness of the causes: the emotions themselves were genuine and great, on a par with the mighty passions of love and hunger. And side by side with the quarrels, communal life generated a touching magnanimity: people were eager to help, support and lend things to one another, and seemed to find affirmation of themselves in helping one another. Each of us was poor, but as proud and generous as millionaires. If one of us baked a cake, most of it would go to our neighbours – not our enemies of course, but our allies, those in our own little group. These groups changed all the time, yesterday's enemy became today's ally, and would be given a generous slice of cake. Even Panka Zykova, whose satanic pride meant that she never joined forces with anyone – even for a couple of days with Anfisa against Kapa, for instance, or vice versa – even proud Panka would occasionally knock on my door, silently put a plate with a slice of cake on the table and withdraw, spurning my thanks.

Life went on, changes happened slowly. We all aged, Ada Efimovna less so than the rest of us; she still believed in the magical powers of love and moved from one imagined romance to another. But she too would sometimes have a fit of the spleen and stop dying her hair, brushing it smooth and saying mysteriously: 'I'm in mourning for my life, I'm unhappy. Chekhov's *Seagull*.'

Kapa Gushchina still worked as a night watch, but she no longer ran about all day as she used to and had long and frequent naps. She lost her old habit of triumphing in quarrels and became quieter in the kitchen . . . Panka Zykova permed her hair, dashed about even more frantically, raising even more wind, and always seemed to be rushing off somewhere on her strong muscular legs.

My own life wasn't too bad at that time. I felt lulled as by a journey. There are people whose greatest pleasure is to travel – no matter where, no matter how, in a train or a car. The world flashes past and they're never bored. I have gone to extremes in this: I can travel without even stirring. I can sit in a chair and life flashes past, bewitching me with its ever-changing scenery. A drop of water hanging overhead sparkles, swells and falls. After it comes another. It's all quite fascinating. A sparrow hops on to the edge of the path. A very old sparrow. It's clear that he has a great soul for such a tiny, delicate little body. Just look at the way he fights his comrade for that worm, angrily pecking him in the shoulder and hopping off again. His beak is ragged along the edges, but it contains a splendid worm. A blessed life!

From time to time I would pass on the street old friends from my former existence. I always found these occasions awkward and difficult. They were embarrassed to see me crippled, down-at-heel and without a profession, and they would sincerely pity me, yet were unable to help me. But I found their pity oppressive and their interests alien. The world I had abandoned now seemed strange to me, like a house in which one has lived long ago and has already forgotten where the front door is . . . They would tell me about other people's destinies. About such-and-such who had seemed so promising in his time but turned out to be an empty shell, barely scraping a living; and about such-and-such who on the contrary had blossomed and now won prizes, went abroad, was enormously successful and had had his photograph in the papers for the past three months, the last one in *Culture and Life* – did I see it? 'No,' I'd reply. My friend would say goodbye, taking his leave of me as of a hopeless invalid, and after each of these meetings I'd ask myself: am I really so deprived? Do I envy them their lives – with all the competitiveness, the succession of foreign trips and newspaper photographs? No, I don't envy them . . . At that time I was rereading Karel Čapek's *English Letters* and I read there as if for the first time a phrase which struck me with its aching musicality: 'Oh my country, which has no seas, are not your horizons too narrow? Perhaps you lack clamorous expanses? Yes, but we have these expanses inside our own heads and if we cannot sail then we can at least dream, furrow vast worlds in our own flights of fancy, make space in this world for ships and journeys . . .'

I had a lot to thank my fate for. I had a job, I had a

home, and I had Anfisa and Vadim. Awkward and ridiculous though it might be, I had a family. For the first time in many years the wall separating my past from the present collapsed and I could at last recall the past without screaming in pain.

These memories often prevented me from sleeping at night, but I wasn't too bothered by my insomnia. I would look with a kind of joy out of the window where the lamp cast its shadow, and I would feel the ship of widows rocking as it sailed on to its unknown but blessed destination.

[17]

From time to time anxiety breaks through my narrative and I cannot go on. Is it really a general law that human relations degenerate with the years and savage flesh grows over living tissue? The gnawing question is when did this happen? Not yet anyway. Everything was still all right then, I think. Anfisa and I worked and Vadim went to school. His work was so-so. He didn't work particularly well or badly, just sullenly. I think he was deeply hurt by the realisation that he wasn't the best. In fact his whole life after the House of the Child was a downward path from best to second best. As he grew up he became less beautiful too: he grew coarser and fatter and began to stoop slightly. He had Anfisa's large bones. For her he was still a god though, and she spoilt him wildly. She worked 'two deaths', as she put it – in other words two shifts. Then she applied for a third death, washing linen and cleaning windows. She did it all for him. Clothes, shoes, vitamins, fruit, theatre, cinema – it was all for him. She herself became shabbier and shabbier, went without new clothes and started looking like an old woman. Yet Vadim was so cold and unaffectionate. You'd kiss him and he'd wipe his face. She'd go up to him and he'd say: 'Leave me alone.' He became more and more insolent, and developed the habit of hanging his head with a sullen look.

'Don't you dare butt me!' Kapa would say. 'I'm not afraid of you!' And Vadim would smirk. He always smirked, whatever people said to him. He teased the cat and shot at things with a catapult. Once he broke a window. His mother paid for the glass and wept – and he smirked. They were just the usual boyish pranks, but that mocking smirk of his was very unusual.

Then his relationship with the children in the courtyard became somewhat complicated. Someone hurt him badly, evidently by saying the cruel word 'bastard' to him. And he heard things from people who knew that not everything in his family had run smoothly . . .

I don't remember when I first heard from him his famous phrase 'they're making it all up'. 'You make it up, and she makes it up ("she" was his mother), and everyone makes it up,' he said to me.

'Aren't you ashamed of yourself, Vadim? What d'you mean, she's making it up? She dotes on you, she loves you more than her own life.'

'She's always making things up. She does it deliberately. She gives me potatoes with cream, and has hers without. She's poor but she pretends not to be so people will think she's rich.'

'Where on earth do you get words like rich and poor from, Vadim? We don't have rich or poor people, it's simply easier for some and harder for others, that's all.'

'Well, Kolka Lokhmatov brought a salmon sandwich to school, and took one bite and threw it away. And you tell me he's not rich? And the teacher makes things up too.'

He was utterly caught up in his 'they're all making it

up', like one bewitched. And once he had acquired this simple idea he considered himself quite superior to others. He spoke about Anfisa with contempt, forgave her nothing, resented everything: her quarrel with Kapa, her tears, the fact that she washed floors for money, and mainly the fact that she made things up. It was useless trying to dissuade him, it would only make him more adamant. Once he said with the terrifying intonation of the dead Fyodor: 'She suffocates me.'

He didn't often refer to his father, but it was obvious that he remembered him and loved him. He would recall how they used to go to the zoo, or how Fyodor had made him a little gun which shot peas.

Once Vadim said to me, in a far too adult tone, like the collective voice of the flat: 'You're always defending her but I know better. Father was killed because of her. He wanted to live but she wouldn't let him. That's why he drank.'

'What a perfectly horrible thing to say, Vadim. Who told you that?'

'No one told me, I just know.'

But I didn't want to argue with him. I just wanted to understand him . . .

* *

I shall never forget the day when Vadim learnt that Fyodor wasn't his real father. He had overheard a conversation between Kapa and Ada Efimovna and he ran up to me pale and shaking, his forehead beaded with sweat. He clung to me like a baby: 'What are they saying? What are they saying in there? They said papa wasn't my real father!'

I said nothing. I wanted to say 'they're making it all up' but couldn't bring myself to. Vadim sobbed, shouting: 'You're not denying it! It must be true then!'

I stood over him, not knowing how to comfort him. He sobbed desperately, throwing his head back and forth, and at each movement his little Adam's apple trembled. The violence of his grief astonished me. For some reason I tried to prise his clenched fingers away from his face so that I could see it. When I succeeded he bit my hand. My God, I hadn't helped him at all, I hadn't managed to get through to him. I put my bitten hand in my mouth. He leapt up like a wild animal and rushed to the door.

'I'll never come and see you again, so there!'

Later that evening Anfisa came in and cried: 'How spiteful people are! Why do they have to torment a child like that? We never did them any harm!'

'They didn't do it on purpose – he just happened to overhear them . . .'

'Oh yes they did! Kapa's had it in for me for a long time now. I have a son and hers is dead. And your Ada is also a proper shrew. She's envious of me for having a son too. So they've both been plotting together to take my son away from me . . .'

'That's not true, Anfisa Maximovna, you shouldn't slander people like that.'

'So you're standing up for them, are you? They've behaved vilely and you try to defend them? That's great! So now we know – they mean more to you than I do!'

She stopped crying and left the room. This time she shut herself in for a long time, and when she passed Kapa and me on her way to the kitchen she turned aside. She refused to do my cleaning for me. Now Kapa did it instead, and on the days when she washed the floor Anfisa would become like a madwoman and kick over the pail of water. One day I hung up my underwear on her washing-line as usual, and came back to find it torn to shreds on my kitchen table, which was filthy.

'Well you see it's . . .' I said, pouring water on the table with shaking hands and wiping it clean.

'Hang your things on my line, don't be embarrassed,' said Kapa. 'I don't grudge you my washing-line!'

So I hung things there instead. What a business!

A raging storm of communal passions. I suffered, and Anfisa suffered. I was right, and she was right.

Somewhere in all this complexity I lost sight of Vadim. He had stopped coming in to see me and whenever he met me in the corridor he would hang his head and scowl. I didn't try to win him back – I was too proud, damned fool that I was! Fancy getting on my high horse with a child! I can never forgive myself for that. Because it was then that I lost Vadim. Anfisa gradually, slowly, returned. But not Vadim.

Poor boy, how he must have longed to unburden his heart if he started visiting Ada Efimovna! The first time I discovered he was doing so I was stricken with jealousy. Ada's room was next to mine. Once I heard her guttural chirping and her mermaid laugh – clearly she had someone in there with her. A man . . . ? No, I realised it must be Vadim. He burst out with some passionate utterance, and I recognised his voice and the words 'they're all making it up'. And she laughed. She didn't contradict him, she laughed. I struck my fist on the windowsill and didn't notice that I'd hurt my hand. That was stupid – I had to take care of my hands.

From then on Vadim began to visit Ada regularly and to avoid me. Maybe he was ashamed of his outburst and didn't know how to smoothe it over. More likely he actually needed Ada more than me at this difficult time. I was too complicated, too serious. He was instinctively drawn to her, like a dog instinctively knowing what sort of grass to eat . . .

[18]

That evening was almost the first time Vadim had visited

Ada. He knocked at her door.

'Who's there? Oh well come in, I'm already dressed.'

Vadim went in. 'Is it all right?'

'Of course it is, what a question! Do whatever you want. Sit down, I'll be finished in a moment.'

Ada Efimovna was standing in front of the mirror putting the last touches to her face. Then she finished and turned to Vadim. 'Don't you think I'm rather piquant?'

'I don't know what that means.'

'Oh, but you must understand about beauty. Beauty is the very essence of the spiritual life.'

Vadim liked that bit about the essence. Ada Efimovna's room was funny, like a plaything. Funny curtains with hares on them, like in the nursery school, and on a rug in the corner was a gigantic doll, with outstretched arms.

'That's Alisa,' said Ada Efimovna, 'Some admirer sent her. She's from abroad. She closes her eyes and speaks. See for yourself.'

Vadim looked and sure enough she opened her eyes, closed her eyes and spoke from her stomach – it sounded a bit like 'mama', only it wasn't in Russian.

Vadim rather enjoyed playing with the doll for a while, but he quickly came to his senses.

'What d'you want a doll for – you're a grown-up!' he said.

'But grown-ups need to play too. What is this life for? Why, life is a game.' She sang the last words, rolling her eyes.

Vadim liked that too. It was true – life was a game. Games were almost the same as lies, only more fun.

They talked of various things: about school, and marks, and Bars the cat, which Vadim had again tied by the tail to the door of the lavatory. Someone had gone in there and the cat had howled. Ada screwed up her deep-set little eyes and screamed with laughter. 'Oh Vadim, how could you be so cruel!'

It was so easy with Ada. They would drink tea and eat sweets and look at the photos on the walls, which were all papered. The photos were mostly portraits of Ada Efimovna herself in various roles: with a fan, in a top hat and in a striped bathing-suit. There were also portraits of various men, with moustaches and without moustaches, with capes and without capes, and they all had their mouths open and were singing.

'My friends from the stage,' explained Ada Efimovna. 'The stage is a world of its own. You don't understand that yet, but you will.'

'Who's that fat man over there?' asked Vadim. He particularly disliked the man with the spreading belly and gaping mouth.

'That was my first husband. He was not fat, merely stout and imposing. Stoutness doesn't harm a man, it's a woman who has to watch her figure.'

'Did he die?'

'What are you talking about? He still sings – he's a distinguished artist!' She told Vadim his surname, which meant absolutely nothing to him.

'Why did Kapa say you were a widow then?'

'That was from my third husband. He did die, although he'd abandoned me before that. All these experiences made me lose my voice. And what a voice I had! Pure silver!' Ada Efimovna looked a little sad for a moment, then burst out laughing again. 'You're still young, you don't know what it means to pine for the past. But why be sad? Life is beautiful! There are so many joys – music, love, nature, architecture . . .'

Vadim found it both tedious and enjoyable to listen to her.

'Well I'll be off then. Thanks for the tea and the sweets.'

'Don't mention it. Come again. If only you knew how lonely I am . . .'

When Vadim had left Ada Efimovna started getting

ready for bed. This was a serious business and took over two hours of her time every day. First she made the bed, plumped up the pillows and neatly laid out her lacey nightdress. Then came her ablutions, with three kinds of skin cream and various lotions. Then she put a glass of sweet tea and some biscuits on the bedside table, for she liked to nibble something sweet when she woke up in the middle of the night.

When she had finished her preparations she got into bed. But she didn't go to sleep: she was thinking of Vadim. A fine boy, but so bitter. She too might have had such a son if she hadn't had one of those abortions . . . Her life, dedicated only to herself, now filled her with horror. What had that life contained? Love? No, there'd been no real love. She had been eager to love someone truly, to the grave, but circumstances had not permitted it – she had been perpetually rejected and deceived. As she remembered her past, which contained no love, only men and abortions, Ada Efimovna wept bitterly . . . .

Vadim started visiting more and more frequently. At first he was shy, then he grew more confident with her. She was funny, but kind.

Anfisa was against it. 'Why d'you have to make friends with her? She's got neither brains nor commonsense – she's just like someone out of a musical comedy show. I never minded when you used to visit the other one, Flerova, did I? She's a serious person, she's a composer.'

But Vadim paid no attention and continued to visit Ada rather than Olga Ivanovna; he found her so much easier to be with. 'Everything will be all right,' she would croon to him.

Sometimes she would put on an old gramophone record of one of her operatic arias: 'Listen, pure silver, isn't it!' The record would turn and squeak, and the distant voice of the young Ada would pour out its song, while old Ada sat beside it, tonelessly accompanying herself under her breath. Vadim listened to the two Adas sing, and strangely enough he liked it. He had a patronising attitude to Ada, unlike his attitude to other people, including his mother. Gradually he became bolder and freer with her, and began talking to her about the fact that everyone made things up.

'Yes indeed,' nodded Ada, 'You're quite right, there's a lot of lying in this life. Happiness is a lie, love is a lie . . .'

'I didn't mean that. I just wanted to know why everyone made things up all the time.'

'Do I?' Ada Efimovna asked flirtatiously, her little eyes disappearing into her cheeks.

'Of course you do. Why do you dye your hair? Your hair's grey.'

'But Vadim,' said Ada Efimovna in a hurt voice, 'you can't call the desire to be beautiful lying!'

'Well, all right,' agreed Vadim magnanimously. 'But what about her? Why does she always make things up then?' ('She' was his mother.)

Ada Efimovna had no special liking for Anfisa Maximovna at the time, yet even she felt obliged to stand up for her: 'You mustn't talk about your mother like that! She's devoted her whole life to you!'

'But I don't need that! Why did she have me in the first place? I didn't ask her to. She bought me some new trousers when she didn't have anything to wear herself. I deliberately burnt them with a cigarette.'

'So you smoke already, do you!'

'We all do it. We hide in the lavatories and do it on the quiet.'

'So you tell lies too!' laughed Ada Efimovna.

'No I don't. I do it in the open. One of the old birds found out once and made a terrible racket: "A-a-h! A boy's smoking!" And she dragged me off to see the headmistress. But I'm not afraid of her. What can she do to me? She's scared to death of any sort of carry-on – the school's top in the district and she doesn't want it to lose its place. She's even scared of me! "Gromov, I have to have a serious talk with you!" she says and her eyes are darting all over the place. So I say to her straight out: "Your're scared of me, aren't you!" And that was the end of her! I had a good laugh and went out. So they didn't touch me . . . They're all the same, they all make things up . . . '

'What's made you so disillusioned?' said Ada Efimovna. 'You're like Byron.' Vadim was quite proud to be compared to Byron.

[19]

One summer Vadim went off to pioneer camp while Anfisa Maximovna stayed in the city with the nursery school: many of the children had been taken to their parents' dachas, so one could almost say that she was having a rest.

One day an unexpected guest arrived out of the blue to see her – the political education officer from her army days, the same man who had sent her home from the front. He had changed, but she still recognised him.

'Hello there, Gromova,' he said in a cheerful military voice. 'I've come to pay you a little visit. I hope you won't turn me away!'

'Come in, come in, Vasilii Sergeevich! What are you talking about! I'm . . . '

He was getting on, but his manner was still firm and authoritative. He came into the room and looked around.

'So how are you getting on?'

'Fine.'

'Good for you. You just carry on like that too! What did you have, girl or boy?'

'A little boy.'

'Good for you, Gromova. Well I kept your address and thought I'd just look you up, see how you were doing and whether you were doing your duty!'

Anfisa found it both strange and rather alarming that the political education officer should have come on a tour of inspection. She laid the table, ran out for a bottle and had quite a bit to drink. He drank too, and grew sad and talkative. He talked about himself. He had retired now and was living on a pension. It was a lonely life. His wife had died and his daughter had grown up and got married to a border guard at a prohibited zone. He could have moved in with them of course – his daughter and son-in-law wouldn't have turned him away. But he didn't feel ready to be just a grandfather. He still wanted to work, do a bit of good, as they say. He had come to Moscow on his way back to see his daughter, so he thought he'd look in on Anfisa and see how she was doing and talk about the old days.

They spent the evening reminiscing to their hearts' content, and they sang songs, the songs they'd loved so much at the front. His baritone voice was still strong although Anfisa's alto was slightly thin and reedy now. They recalled their army comrades, both those that had lived and those that had perished. He'd kept in touch with many of them. The chief surgeon, the one who was so angry with Anfisa for getting pregnant, had become a great man, an academician. He ran a clinic and did heart operations, and people even visited him from the capitalist countries. Klava the nurse had become a doctor, an otolaryngolist (hard to pronounce at first!), a successful woman and mother of three, who hadn't abandoned her work. They recalled hospital life, the 'Second Front' tins of meat, the bombs, and how terrified Anfisa had been . . .

'But you were a heroine all the same,' he said. 'Oh yes Fisa, you were a heroine all right!'

Anfisa was embarrassed and hid her hands. She spoke

hesitantly, twisting her mouth to conceal the gap where she had a missing tooth. By the end of the evening she'd grown bolder and even began cautiously to smile. 'You're a first-class woman too!' he said. 'One could easily fall in love with a woman like you. Are you planning to get married?'

'What are you talking about, Vasilii Sergeevich? Me get married? Why, I'm an old woman already!'

'Well, even old women get married sometimes, you know!'

He sat there joking with her a bit longer, then left. Next day he called on her again, and he was soon visiting her regularly. Little by little Anfisa got used to him and he got used to her. There was no talk of love, they obviously weren't young any more. It was simply that he liked being with Anfisa and she liked being with him.

In the flat of course they soon started commenting on the fact that she'd moved in a lodger – you can't keep that sort of thing hidden for long. There was no end to the speculations. Olga Ivanovna occasionally listened to what the others said about Anfisa in the kitchen. Kapa spoke straight to Anfisa's face though: 'Sin will burn you, Anfisa. At your age you should be thinking about your soul, not men.'

'Oh, you're always so pious!' snapped Anfisa.

'I'm not pious at all, I'm full of sin, but at least I pray to God to forgive me. And you should pray too.'

'Religion's the opium of the people,' said Anfisa, pleased at this neat rebuff.

'And you're a silly fool,' retorted Kapa, 'jabbering on about things you don't understand. Religion's opium, but you're a copium.' Anfisa had no idea what a 'copium' was, but it sounded very insulting.

Only Ada Efimovna sympathised with Anfisa; she talked endlessly to her about her speciality: 'I'm so happy for you, Anfisa, with my whole heart. Love is an intoxicating dream . . . When I was with Boris . . . '

'Which one was that?'

'I don't remember. The first maybe. No, the second.'

Panka Zykova threw things around and demanded that Anfisa pay for the light and gas per person, that is for three people, quite forgetting that it was she who had once demanded that they pay per room.

With Olga Ivanovna Anfisa was going through what might be called a period of estrangement: they had quarrelled over something and hadn't made it up. It now seemed to her as though Olga Ivanovna was pursuing her with stern eyes and judging her . . . But why should she judge her? Wasn't she a woman too?

The education officer got used to staying with Anfisa; he felt warm and comfortable with her. He kept urging her to marry him, but she simply couldn't bring herself to consent – she worried about how Vadim would take it. But she didn't actually refuse either. Vasilii Sergeevich didn't rush her, but behaved with great confidence: he mended the light, put a new tap in the kitchen and even started to look for a job. And the others in the flat gradually got used to him being there; at least there was a man around the house now . . .

Meanwhile Vadim was pining away at his summer camp. Why was he the only one who was here for two months? He was sick and tired of the place . . . He couldn't bear camp life – all those parades and drums and ridiculous processions, and everyone pretending to enjoy it so much when in fact they were all bored to death. He didn't get on with his comrades either. He thought they were stupid – he preferred not to notice the fact that many of them were actually far more intelligent than he was. He often walked around the camp site on his own. Strangely enough, he thought frequently of his mother. He remembered her sitting in the House of the Child surrounded by babies, gleaming gold in the sunlight, with a crown of dandelions on her head. He remembered her plump, graceful arms shining in the sun, and for the first time in his life he missed his mother and longed to see her again.

Once the director of the camp went into town and took him too. All the way there Vadim was thinking how pleased his mother would be to see him! She'd cry and beam and kiss him. A man didn't need that sort of tenderness of course – he'd simply pat her shoulder.

Arriving back in a state of great excitement, he met Kapa on the stairs.

'Aah, so you're back. What a nice surprise!'

From Kapa's cheerful face and sly glance it was obvious that something was up.

'What d'you mean?'

'Nothing, nothing. You'll see for yourself.'

Vadim went in the room and there was his mother sitting at the table all dressed up, and beside her was a completely strange man. They were having dinner together. His mother leapt up from the table: 'Vadik! I never expected you! What a lovely surprise!' But her eyes were nervous.

'There's no such name as Vadik.'

'Are you back for good, or just visiting?'

'Just visiting.'

The man got up and Vadim looked at his stern aged face. 'Vadim, let me introduce you to Vasilii Sergeevich – we knew each other in the war.'

Vadim didn't offer his hand, just nodded his head and growled something inaudible.

'Sit down and eat something,' Anfisa fussed. 'Let me heat something up for you. It won't take a minute.'

She went out. Vadim sat down and put his fists on the table. Vasilii Sergeevich sat there in front of him. 'I don't want any,' said Vadim.

'What don't you want?'

'I don't want anything. I said I didn't want any and I don't.'

The education officer stared at him. 'Well, you are a

lemon!'

'Good enough to eat, eh?' Vadim smiled insolently. He wanted to cry.

'Don't you think your mother has a right to a life of her own?'

'No.'

'A real lemon,' repeated the education officer. Vadim smiled again and Anfisa came in.

'There darling, you eat that.'

'I don't want any. You two can have it.' And he made for the door.

Anfisa rushed after him: 'Vadik, Vadik!'

The education officer held her back: 'Why are you chasing after him, silly woman?'

'He's my son,' Anfisa shouted.

That night they lay silently in bed together, and next morning Vasilii Sergeevich said: 'Right, I've enjoyed my stay, but I've had enough now, I'm off home.'

'Vasya!'

'That's right, I'm off. It's obvious things would never have worked out for us. You can't control that son of yours, can you! Or can you?' Anfisa said nothing. 'So you can't,' he said. 'So it's all over between us. Full stop.'

Next day he left. Anfisa saw him off, sobbing. But she realised that it had to be.

Vadim returned that autumn heavily sunburnt, and his face looked different somehow.

[20]

So that's what happens: you bring up a son and he becomes a stranger to you.

As Vadim approached manhood he quarrelled more

and more with his mother. He had one phrase that he kept repeating: 'I don't need it.'

'I've ironed your trousers Vadim, here they are.'

'I don't need them.'

'I do everything for you, I work my fingers to the bone for you.'

'Well, I don't need you to do everything for me.'

'Well, if you don't need it I don't either. If you treat me like that I'll treat you the same and see how you like it!'

They didn't speak for two days. Vadim went off God knows where, and came back only to sleep. He smoked too. 'You're still much too young to smoke!' Anfisa Maximovna shouted. 'Earn your own living first, then you can smoke!'

'Ah, so you begrudge me your bread! That's just great! I've had enough! I won't eat here any more with you!' And he didn't. He didn't eat for one day, two days. On the third day Anfisa Maximovna grovelled and apologised to him, 'Forgive me, Vadik. It's all my fault. Smoke if you want, just don't come to any harm.'

He growled something, sat down at the table and ate in a completely indifferent manner, although it was obvious he was very hungry indeed. He ate his fill and shot out of the house: 'Well I'm off now.'

And nobody liked to ask where either. Sometimes he would come back to sleep and sometimes he wouldn't. Anfisa Maximovna would stand at the hall door in her bare feet, listening to every footstep on the stairs – but no, it wasn't him. She wouldn't sleep all night and would get up exhausted to go off to work. That evening Vadim would return home only to start taunting her all over again. Each taunt and jibe would make her hands shake and she'd throw a fit and hurl things on the floor. She was quite indiscriminate: she smashed a whole pile of dessert plates once. That scared Vadim, but he quickly mastered himself, jeered and walked over the broken pieces.

Sometimes Anfisa would say to him: 'Why don't you

and I try to get on better together, like civilised human beings?'

'Why not? I don't care,' replied Vadim. 'I'm quite civilised.'

Anfisa would complain to Olga Ivanovna (they were friends again): 'He despises me, oh how he despises me!'

'Why should he despise you?'

'For the same old thing – Vasilii.'

'But it's horrible of him to despise you!' said Olga Ivanovna pursing her lips. She probably felt that Vadim despised her too. Olga Ivanovna didn't love Vadim any more, and even the chirping Ada had started to fear him – he could be terribly cruel.

But for Anfisa, he was her son, come what may.

[21]

No, I hadn't stopped loving Vadim, he was still very dear to me for some reason. I had put too much into him to let him go without a struggle.

It was partly my own fault too. After he started going in to see Ada Efimovna I, in my stupid vanity, left him alone for a while. He didn't have to visit me if he didn't want to. That was when I lost him. Later on I thought better of it, but by then it was too late, I'd lost him. And I never managed to get through to him after that.

Sometimes I would invite him in to see me. He would refuse, saying : 'I haven't got time.' And if I insisted he would come in, sit on the edge of the bed and say: 'Yes?' That meant: 'All right, let's see what tricks you're up to now!'

I tried to talk to him about school, about life, about books. But he just sneered at everything I said, in a contemptuous, aloof manner. He had acquired a new word: 'pyramidon'. That was his word for lofty sentiments, tender emotions, notions of conscience, duty and love. If you told him something he would screw up his eyes and drawl, distinctly drawing out each syllable: 'py-ra-mi-don'.

He especially disliked talking about books: they reminded him of literature lessons at school, which he considered one long 'pyramidon'. They taught literature 'through images', and it made him gnash his teeth with rage.

'What do I care about the image of Liza Kalitina in *The Nest of the Gentry*? I don't give a damn for that stinking nest. She ohs and ahs and goes off to a convent – and I have to study that rubbish! Pah!'

I tried as best I could to tell him about the depths and charms of Russian literature. I spoke incoherently, searching for words, constantly fearing to lapse into 'pyramidon' and constantly doing so. I had wept over Tolstoy and Turgenev as a young girl – was I really incapable of conveying those tears, that delight, to another person? Vadim would look at me and sneer. When I fell silent he would ask sardonically: 'Can I go now?'

'Yes, Vadim, do.'

Discussions about his mother he tended to avoid altogether, and after the episode with the education officer he stopped talking about her completely, as though she wasn't living in the flat – as though she didn't exist. Once I carefully led the conversation round to this dangerous subject and mentioned Vasilii Sergeevich. The hatred on Vadim's face was so fierce that it frightened me.

'He called me a lemon!'

'So what, maybe he was just joking? And maybe you provoked it!'

'He called me a lemon! You shouldn't call a person that!'

[22]

Vadim had finished the ninth class and gone up to the tenth when Svetka appeared. It happened on a state farm where the whole class had gone to weed vegetables. It was hard work – the earth was dry as a brick but the weeds poked through it like spiteful, bristling hair. Here and there amongst the weeds poked pale green carrot fronds, and the children would pull them out of the earth to expose their puny little pink tails. They'd clean them and try to eat them, but they were limp and dry and they'd throw them out along with the beet tops. It was clear that the field had been ploughed and sown and was now being weeded not so that things could grow there but simply to keep the books straight. Vadim saw the same lying here that pursued him everywhere else, but now it no longer hurt him, it merely made him gloat. It was like he said – people were always making things up. His comrades didn't support him in discussions on this subject – all this talk about lying bored them to death. They simply joked and weeded and gnawed at the carrot tails and threw them away with the tops. Lying didn't trouble them, it wasn't something that hurt them. Vadim felt he was superior to them, cleverer and more statesmanlike in his thinking. But he also envied their cheerful communal spirit. He was always on his own while they enjoyed themselves swimming, roasting potatoes, singing round the camp fire. He went swimming and ate potatoes too, but without enjoyment, merely with a sense of his lofty mission in life. In the evenings it would grow cool, the mosquitoes would buzz and a fine moon would appear in the blue sky. The children would light bonfires, strum guitars, swat at mosquitoes and laugh. 'What on earth are they laughing at?' Vadim would wonder. Yet he was envious.

One evening he was sitting by the bonfire, feeling its heat on his face and stirring the embers with a long charred branch whose black horns resembled a sly devil. He scorched the devil and knocked off its horns, then felt someone tapping his shoulder: 'Let's beat it!' said Svetka.

He looked at her for the first time. What an insignificant little creature she was, just like a white mouse, with a sharp little nose and sharp little teeth. Pretty though.

Bending her scratched childish knees and half-squatting beside Vadim she put her little hand into his big rough one and said again: 'Come one, let's beat it!'

'Good idea!' Vadim wanted to say, but instead he got up, stretched and walked along the dusty blue path with Svetka towards the forest. The bright moon hung overhead and a bird cried out plaintively.

'What's she on about?' said Vadim.

'She's probably looking for her children,' said Svetka quietly. Her dark eyelashes made large shadows on her cheeks and she suddenly seemed very beautiful to him. The forest, the moon, the strange bird searching for her children – it was all so new, so mysterious, so primaeval. And newest of all was the sweet chill around his heart. Shyly Vadim took Svetka's arm. Her slender elbow yielded to him with frightening alacrity. The chill around his heart turned to a feeling of constraint, as though something was pressing down on him. As they approached the forest the path wound sharply to the right, into the darkness of the arched interlaced trees, and Vadim realised that here amongst the trees one could find a respite from lying. They stopped at the edge of the forest and she raised her truthful, indistinct face to his.

'Well, what is it?' he asked.

'I noticed you ages ago,' she said. 'You're interesting.'
'Yes but . . . '

'Don't deny it. You're the most interesting in the group. Maybe even in the whole of the ninth class. Only Vovka Sukhanov's more interesting than you.'

Vadim ground his teeth. He couldn't bear Vovka Sukhanov, that pink and white ninny – more like a sponge-cake with cream than a real boy. And what was more, he was top of the class. He was good at his work, he was good at sport, he was public-spirited, he wrote clever compositions, he spoke at meetings, he lied and he lied and he lied . . .

'Oh well, if he's more interesting than me . . . ' Vadim said roughly.

Svetka moved towards him and flung her arms round his neck: 'Don't be offended. I was just speaking objectively. Now subjectively . . .'

Subjectively, she kissed him. The chill around his heart turned to ice, the bitter moon rolled off to one side and there was only Svetka left in the whole world, her slender body trustingly stretching up to him on tiptoe.

* *

The days at the state farm flashed past. Before this Vadim had hated them, counted them on his fingers, longed for them to end. Now he counted the days too, but he dreaded them passing. If only he could halt them! Every evening he and Svetka, ignoring the others' smirks, would go off hand in hand to the forest. There, under the wide-apart, shaggy-pawed fir trees, was their only true home. Vadim carried in his pocket an oil-cloth their 'domestic comfort'. It had a wonderful, fresh, synthetic smell which made Vadim's head reel. He'd furtively sniff the smell off his fingers during the day, and in the evenings it would blossom and mingle with the innocent chicken-like smell of her bright hair. Each time he embraced Svetka and inhaled the smell of her hair

Vadim's heart would be filled with pain. He wanted to forget the fact that everyone lied. Maybe they did, but so what? And the days continued to rush on, however much he beseeched them to slow down. The thin moon grew wide, round and ripe, then got thinner on one side and started to wane again: 'Watch it skew-face!' Vadim threatened. The moon was robbing him. And Svetka too was being troublesome. Once again she quite gratuitously mentioned Vovka Sukhanov. Vadim hit her. She burst into tears: 'How horrible you are, how rude and rough!'

Vadim was appalled by what he'd done but tried to keep a grip on himself.

'How could you hit a woman!' Svetka sobbed.

'Why shouldn't I?' said Vadim. 'That's nineteenth-century morality that says you can't hit a woman. Look at those Italian films – they swipe a woman just for having a pretty face in them!'

Svetka raised her eyes to him, her eyelashes trembling with tears. 'But in those films they hit women because they love them so much. They love them to distraction, that's why they hit them.'

'But I love you, Svetka!' said Vadim. 'I love you to distraction, that's why I hit you. Forgive me, forgive me. Hit me back if you want. I've gone crazy!'

The tears on her cheeks were salty. She snuggled up to him again – that meant she'd forgiven him. She kissed him – that meant she loved him. 'Forgive me, forgive me,' he kept mumbling. 'I'm mad about you.'

* *

But there's no understanding women. Next day she was very cool with him and refused to leave the camp fire. The day after that too. She sang to the guitar with the others, as though making fun of him. Vadim was miserable. He invited red-haired Maika, the basketball-player, out for a walk, just to spite her. (Maika was the tallest girl in the class and looked like a boy with an accordion.) But he didn't get anywhere with her. He tried to kiss her but she just offered him her ear. They walked back. 'You think you're the Sad Princess,' muttered Vadim to himself. Svetka was sitting by the camp fire, screwing up her eyes and smiling, as though she couldn't care less that he was walking with Maika.

The day soon came when they had to leave and he and Svetka still hadn't had a talk. It rained all that morning, a fine, cold driving rain. The young people took their seats in the trucks, and when Svetka scrambled in over the big wheels she looked so small and unhappy. He helped her in and squeezed her cold childish leg. She just stared coldly at him and drew back her leg. Well, let her sulk. Vadim didn't need her.

Vadim had no raincoat. He could have done with his 'domestic comfort' now, but he'd thrown it away the other day in order to get rid of the smell. It was raining and the others offered him a tarpaulin to wrap around himself, but he wouldn't take it and deliberately got soaked, hoping to catch pneumonia and die and go to the devil.

The city was exactly the same as before – the same hateful flat, the same room, the same mother.

'How big and handsome you've grown, my boy!' she said, shyly delighted to see him. 'I wouldn't have recognised you.'

And she cried of course – he knew she would.

'Crying again! I can't bear it! Women's tears – lies! Here you are blubbering away – can't you see I'm soaked to the skin, woman? Give me some dry things!'

Anfisa fussed and commiserated and fetched him some dry clothes, while he sat there sullenly, thinking how much he'd like to die. But he didn't die, he didn't even fall ill.

He went back to school. And everything there was exactly the same too. Svetka seemed remote, and rather ugly too: her little face was careworn and her mouth was wrinkled. She smiled at him but Vadim frowned back. Let her wag her tail and wait for him to approach her. She'd never wait that long!

Over a month passed before Svetka herself arranged a meeting. 'Come to the square tomorrow after school,' she said, 'the bench by the war memorial.'

Vadim nodded. At first he decided not to go, to punish her a bit more, but then he decided he would. She was already there, sitting on the bench, hanging her head and kicking stones with her toes, which poked out of her open sandals.

'Well, what d'you want?' asked Vadim. He loved her again.

'Hello there,' said Svetka. 'I've got to talk to you.'

She looked in a bad way. Her hair wasn't spreading over her shoulders but pinned up on top of her head, revealing her ears.

'Well, hurrry up and tell me,' said Vadim hoarsely. 'I don't have all day.'

Svetka burst into tears. Women's tears again, damn it! First his mother, now her. His love was beginning to wane again.

'Don't howl. Tell me what the matter is.' (A man must be stern, it said in some book.)

'I can't just like that, all at once – I'm embarrassed.'

'She'll probably say, "I love you"' thought Vadim, his heart pounding, and his love grew again. These wild swings from love to hate and back again were sheer torture. He was sweating. For God's sake, hurry up and say 'I love you' . . .

Svetka opened her mouth, gulped and said: 'Oh Vadik, I think I've fallen –'

'How d'you mean, fallen?'

'Like other women fall, of course! Don't you understand – one little person's made another little person!' She stopped crying and looked at him, dry-eyed, with a look of hatred.

'I haven't done anything, I don't understand!'

'You understood then!' she said with fierce loathing.

She was quite terrifying, with her peasant-woman's bun and her small dry eyes. There could be no talk of love now. What did she want of him? Get married? In the tenth class? Impossible! And what would he tell his mother?

'What shall we do then?' he said, avoiding her eyes.

She said nothing.

'Get married or what?'

Svetka burst out laughing: 'Married! Look at you, a snivelling little husband you'd make!'

'Well, what shall we do then?'

'What everyone else does when they fall. I've already made arrangements with someone, she'll do it cheap.' She named a sum of money. Vadim was stunned. 'I've got half of that, I need the other half. I thought you . . . '

'But I don't have it, Svetka . . .'

'Get it off your mother then.'

'She won't give it – besides she doesn't have it either.'

'Well, get it somewhere else. You're a man.'

Vadim felt mortally depressed. 'All right, I'll try.'

'And be quick about it. I need it by Friday. She wants it in advance, and today's Tuesday.'

'I said I'd try. I'll see you later.'

'So long,' said Svetka, in English for some reason, and waved her hand in the foreign manner, with the palm outwards.

Vadim ground his teeth. What mountains of lies!

In the end he got the money from Ada Efimovna. He had to tell her everything, she wouldn't have given it otherwise. Ada was horrified, but delighted too. 'Did you love her, dear, did you truly love her?'

'Yes, I truly loved her.'

'My poor children! But you must give me your word that this will be the last time!' He promised readily – he himself was appalled by the mess he'd got himself into.

On Thursday he took the money to Svetka. On Friday she didn't come to school, and she didn't come on Saturday either. Vadim was beside himself with anxiety and remorse. He imagined the worst: Svetka had died, or had told her mother everything, and her mother was now rushing over to complain . . . All Saturday and Sunday he was in a state of despair, but on Monday she came back to school as though nothing had happened, not even looking pale, and with her hair spread out over her shoulders again. She never stopped lying. Vadim swore never to love anyone ever again.

[23]

The tenth class passed quickly, and eventually, stumbling over the lessons as though they were hummocks, Vadim finished school and brought home his certificate. It was so-so, mainly threes. Anfisa Maximovna read it and burst into tears: 'What can we do now? Who'll take you with that certificate? It was my dream that you'd go to the institute one day – but that's out of the question now.'

For all the other children in the building the day was a holiday. They'd left school after all, even if they did have threes. For Vadim though it was nothing but tears, and he found these tears unbearable.

'But I don't want to go to the institute! Fat lot of good it'd do me slogging away to qualify as an engineer just to earn my living to make money! I'd rather go out to work now, thanks!'

Anfisa burst into loud sobs – she even had an attack of hysteria, like women in pre-revolutionary novels. Vadim spat and went out to the kitchen.

Ada Efimovna was standing by the stove in an apron,

making some kind of sauce. She wasn't really very good at cooking, but every so often she'd make something really unusual. The sauce gurgled in the saucepan.

'What've you got there?' Vadim asked sullenly.

'*Sauce printanière* with white wine. An old recipe. It should be quite something if it doesn't burn.'

Vadim's face expressed the most profound contempt for everything pre-revolutionary, *sauce printanière* included. Ada Efimovna burst out laughing: 'What's the matter? Why are you so cross?'

'I've finished school.'

Ada Efimovna clapped her hands: 'But that's splendid! Well done!'

The sauce had boiled away: 'I knew it would!' she said calmly. 'Domestic things just aren't my forte. I was made for higher nervous activity. What were we saying? Oh yes, congratulations. One great phase of your life is over and a new one has started.'

'I don't give a damn for those phases!' said Vadim.

'Lord, how cynical you are! Are all young people like that now?'

'Even worse!'

'I don't believe it!'

Anfisa Maximovna's sobs were audible now even in the kitchen. 'What's that?' asked Ada in astonishment.

'She's celebrating the end of one great phase of my life – celebrating her son's success.'

'Bad results, eh?'

'Crummy!'

'More cynicism?'

'Sorry, I meant mediocre – twelfth out of thirty.'

'Twelfth, but that's good! From the bottom or the top?'

'From the top unfortunately!'

'But that's good all the same.'

'Well, she thinks it's bad! She says she's dreamt all her life of sending her son to the institute.'

'Well, dreaming's one thing,' said Ada Efimovna,

although it wasn't quite clear what she meant by this.

That evening Olga Ivanovna brought him a present, a case of drawing instruments. Vadim thanked her drily: 'Thanks, but times have changed. No one works in Indian ink now, they all use pencil.'

* *

Vadim didn't go to the graduation party. You had to pay, and he didn't want to ask his mother for the money. What did he need parties for anyway? He spent the evening at home instead, smoking in bed. His mother didn't dare criticise him for smoking now, and merely opened the ventilation window.

Then there was yet more talk about his education, about the institute – what a bore it all was. Vadim eventually couldn't hold out any longer and gave in. He handed in some bits of paper to one of the institutes where there was least competition and started preparing for the entrance exams.

It was a hot, lazy summer with occasional thunderstorms that brought no real relief, and Vadim was in a bad mood as he prepared for his exams. Whoever invented this ridiculous idea of going straight from one set of exams to another? No sooner had he finished school and taken his exams there than he had to take yet another set for the institute. And for the same curriculum, what was more. It was all so pointless, like some sort of grim joke. There was only one thing that mattered: his school-leaving certificate. But this was the worst of both worlds – you had to show them your certificate *and* take an exam.

It wasn't as if he wanted to go in the first place. All he wanted was a quiet life without too much exertion, to work a little and not have to burst a blood vessel making his living. Some lucky people didn't have anyone breathing down their neck to work and study.

These 'lucky people' were always present in Vadim's

thoughts – 'other people', whom he sullenly envied. Not that he thought they were any better than he was, quite the contrary, he merely envied their ability, their unpretentiousness. On the question of his education he yielded to his mother and then felt furious – with her, with himself, and with all those 'lucky people'.

Anfisa Maximovna greeted her son's consent to continue his studies with shy gratitude and leant over backwards to provide the right conditions for him. When the nursery left for the dacha she didn't go and took a temporary job as a cleaner instead for just one wage – she lost out on the pay but what did it matter when her son's future was at stake? She looked after him as though he were an invalid and went around on tiptoe – study my son, study. He studied adequately but not very diligently. He would frequently get up from his table, lie down on his bed and light a cigarette. Shyly going up to him, she would ask him why he was lying down again: 'Your poor head must be aching from all that lying down! Why don't I open the window?'

'You don't have to!'

'But why are you always lying down?'

'I'm thinking!'

'Ah, think then, think . . .'

Anfisa awaited the day of the exams like the Day of Judgement. When they started, each day was like a year for her. She trembled and hoped – she almost prayed! Then Kapa began getting at her on the side: 'There was another poor long-suffering mother, just like you, spent three years pushing her son to go to the institute. She pushed and she pushed but it was no good. Then the priest said to her: "Why don't you pray to Sofia the Wise?" So she did. And her son was accepted. And they'd never have accepted him if she hadn't said those prayers . . . '

Anfisa brushed Kapa aside, but in her heart she whispered: 'God help us, God help us!' She didn't pray though.

For one reason or another the exams went badly and Vadim didn't make the grade – he was two or three marks short.

Afterwards he took to his bed, and just lay there for days on end, smoking and not talking to his mother. All he ever said was: 'Leave me alone, can't you?' What if it was schizophrenia? God forbid!

Anfisa worried herself sick – she just didn't know how to help him. She thought and she thought, then she made up her mind. At the nursery there was a curly-haired little girl in the middle group called Lucy Navolochkina. Someone had told Anfisa that Lucy's grandfather was the dean at the institute where Vadim had taken his exams. And the dean was the big chief. Anfisa decided to visit the dean without telling Vadim. She found out his address and went there. She was terrified, but she'd do anything for her son.

[24]

The house where the dean lived was old and sombre, with a scroll above the door. At the entrance two black marble women held corpulent vases on their heads. Anfisa went in terrified: what if the dean chased her straight down the stairs? Unfortunately the lift wasn't working and she could barely drag herself up to the fifth floor. She had put on a lot of weight over the last few years, and she found it especially difficult to climb stairs and wash floors. Whenever she bent over everything would go black in front of her eyes and her head would spin.

She recovered her breath and rang the bell. The door

was opened by the dean himself, a tall old man with a nose like a rudder and luxuriant eyebrows. He greeted her with old-fashioned courtesy: 'Pray come in.'

'Forgive me sir, I've come to see you on business, I teach at the nursery where your Lucy goes.'

The dean paled: 'Has something happened to her? Tell me at once!'

He took her arm and dragged her into the hall, carefully closing the door into the inner room. 'Tell me, but quietly. My wife, you know, her heart . . .'

'No no,' said Anfisa Maximovna hurriedly. 'Nothing's wrong with Lusenka. She's at the dacha – I'm in the city and the nursery's at the dacha. But everything's all right there, I'd be the first to know if it wasn't.'

'Tell me the truth!'

'That's the honest truth, sir. May the earth swallow me up if I'm lying!'

'I was so terrified! I know I'm just a silly old man, but that curly-haired goose means the world to me. Forgive me.'

'Don't worry, it's my fault. I should have phoned, but I've taken the liberty of . . .' Anfisa Maximovna started weeping. She was already weak from crying.

'Dear oh dear!' said the dean. 'Wailing by the waters of Babylon, eh? Have a good cry, don't mind me, you'll feel better for it. Come on, I'll get you some valerian.'

His study was filled with heavy furniture, heavy curtains and quantities of books. The dean anxiously fussed about by the cupboard, dancing around and muttering under his breath some little verses in which 'valerian' rhymed with 'good fun' and 'basin' and God knows what else. He poured some valerian for both of them and they clinked glasses and drank.

'Why not have a little drink to keep you company? That's the way people become alcoholics, you know! I was going to start howling too, just to keep you company! That would have been a nice picture, eh?! He looked at her affably, moving his rudder-like nose from side to side. His thick eyebrows curled downwards, not upwards, and almost reached his eyes.

'Pray sit down,' he said, indicating a chair. She sat down and so did he. 'Now then, I'm at your service.'

'Like a trial,' thought Anfisa nervously.

'I don't really know how to start. I have a son called Vadim, my only child, born in forty-four. He's just finished secondary school and applied to your institute . . .'

'And?'

'He failed.'

The dean frowned. 'Well, what am I supposed to do about it? This isn't an advice centre and I'm not a nurse . . .'

'I don't know . . . I've . . . I'd just like some advice.'

'It's nothing to do with me, understand?' shouted the dean. 'I have absolutely nothing to do with the selection committee! And even if I did . . .'

'I understand,' said Anfisa Maximovna getting up.

'No you don't, you don't understand anything! Sit down! Oh what an idiot!' He pulled her arm painfully and made her sit down again. 'Maybe you think I'm a heartless old man – that I could help, but I won't? That's what you think, eh?'

Anfisa was frightened. She had been thinking exactly that.

The dean laughed: 'I can read people's minds, you see!'

'I'd better go,' said Anfisa.

She tried again to leave but her chair was so deep and soft she found it difficult to get up.

'Sit down!' The dean silenced her. 'Now you've come you'd better stay. Tell me everything from the beginning. Tell me about your son and why he failed – maybe there was some misunderstanding and we can clear it up . . . ' The door opened a crack and a soft, plump, white-haired old woman peered in and asked: 'Ah, you have guests

Seryozha, am I in your way?'

'Yes, you are!' said the dean fiercely.

The old woman laughed and disappeared. Anfisa felt so envious for some reason. If things had worked out differently for her she too might have knocked at her husband's door and asked: 'Am I in your way?' She had never envied youth, just a peaceful old age.

'So tell me everything!' repeated the dean, folding his arms, settling his nose and almost covering his eyes with their beetling brows. 'In as much detail as possible, please.'

* *

Some two hours later a soothed and cheered Anfisa Maximovna was standing at the bus stop waiting for a bus to take her home. The bus didn't come for a long time but she was glad; it was good to get a bit of fresh air once in a while. There was a lovely pink sky and curly little clouds – she hadn't looked at the sky for such a long time, she never had time, her life was like that . . . And how good Sergei Petrovich and Sofia Vladimirovna were! Some people certainly lived well. Their happiness wasn't a matter of books or furniture, it was a matter of loving one another and living peacefully together. They'd given her tea, and to go with the tea there were knot-shaped pastries so plump and soft they melted in your mouth. She must have baked them herself. Anfisa would like to have asked for the recipe, but she was embarrassed. And Sofia Vladimirovna's hands were so small and soft, like the pastries.

Sergei Petrovich didn't promise anything definite, but she went home feeling so happy. In the bus some fellow said to her: 'What a lovely smile, darling!' He was probably drunk, but it was nice all the same.

She got home. The room was dark – Vadim must have gone out. She put on the light and saw him lying on the bed, his long legs flung over the back and his eyes glaring at the ceiling. In his hands were the remains of an extinguished cigarette.

'Vadik, what's the matter? Are you ill?'

'No.'

'But why are you lying there?'

'Because I want to. Why shouldn't I? Isn't a person allowed to lie down?'

'Yes of course, but if you're tired why not get undressed and have a sleep?'

'Because I don't want to.'

'But you can't lie down like that with all your clothes on and your legs on the bedspread, which your mother will have to wash. My hands aren't state property you know. Hands in the bucket all morning and in the trough all evening.'

'Well, who asked you to do it? I'll wash it myself!'

'Yes, I know how you'll wash it – cigarette in your mouth, one, two and it's done. While your mother works herself into an early grave.'

Vadim sat up on his bed and shouted: 'I don't need you to do everything for me! Understand? Stop doing everything for me!'

He jumped up and started moving towards her with a look of such frenzy on his face that Anfisa Maximovna was terrified. She screamed and began to move away, covering her face with her arms, as though shielding herself from a blow. But Vadim didn't hit her. 'You're always making things up and you're doing it now, as though I wanted to hit you! A fat lot of good it'd do me to dirty my hands by hitting you!'

He grabbed his jacket frantically, fumbling with the sleeves. Eventually he got it on, fiercely buttoned it up and dashed out of the room.

'Vadim, where are you going? Vadim, come back!' But the bird had flown. The door onto the staircase banged shut. 'Brawlers!' said Zykova loudly from the next room. 'That's it! I shall get the tribunal to throw them out!'

Anfisa Maximovna collapsed onto the bed. It was all the same to her that Panka Zykova was on the other side of the wall. Let her grumble. Anfisa Maximovna beat her fist on the wall and made it bleed. She looked at it in astonishment – the pain was so pleasant. Then she struck her head against the wall with all her might. There were tufts of hair in her hands – she tore at it joyfully and soon stopped crying and snarling. She heard her hair being torn out together with the skin from her scalp, and she thought how good it would be to be without a head. She stuffed the blanket into her mouth and started tearing it to shreds . . . Then she felt a cold rain on her head and she froze, with the blanket in her teeth. Water streamed down her collar.

'Anfisa Maximovna dear, what's the matter?' trilled a voice. Ada Efimovna was standing over her in her parrot-coloured dressing gown, her hair in curlers, pouring water over Anfisa's head from a trembling glass.

'Calm yourself, dear, it's just a hysterical fit, they're not so uncommon, I have them too. It's not surprising, considering all you've been through. Take some valerian, it'll soon pass.'

Anfisa Maximovna took the blanket out of her mouth, raised her dishevelled head and said: 'I've already had some thanks.'

'What?'

'Valerian.'

'Well, take something else then. You must take something. I have some salol and belladonna in my medicine chest. D'you want some?'

'Yes, all right,' said Anfisa Maximovna, waving her arm. She now felt ashamed of her sobbing fit. She had let herself go for no good reason.

Ada Efimovna ran off to get the medicine and Olga Ivanovna appeared at the door, thin and wide-eyed, wrapping her dressing gown around her.

'Why not get undressed, Anfisa Maximovna? Let me

help you into bed.' She tried to take off Anfisa's shoes, but Anfisa tucked up her feet.

Ada Efimovna flitted in with the medicine: 'There, gulp that down.'

'Oh, what a fool I am, I've got them all worried now,' thought Anfisa. Her head was buzzing like a mosquito. She wound off her fingers some long, light brown hairs, slightly tinged with grey.

[25]

That night Vadim didn't return home, but he appeared next day, meek as a lamb, and asked whether he could get her some breakfast (she answered 'no'), and for a whole week the only evidence of his existence was a huge pile of cucumbers. That week they were going to put up the lists at the institute. Anfisa Maximovna went there every day, but they kept telling her it was too early. Eventually they appeared. She read them from beginning to end: V. F. Gromov's name wasn't there. 'I knew it, I knew it,' she said through chilled lips, but she still couldn't believe it.

'Enquiries at the selection board,' said someone behind her back, and she felt herself swept along to the selection board, where a large crowd of worried-looking boys and girls and parents all jostled one another. A mother, heavily made up, was sobbing loudly and demanding 'respect for the fathers'. The pale, emaciated president, evidently pushed to the limits of his endurance, waved his arm at her and went out. The queue booed. The secretary tried to keep things under control and to send everyone off in different directions.

'Vladimir Alexandrovich has already left, don't you

understand? He's not receiving any more people today!' The secretary's eyes bulged like a cod. She'd murder you without batting an eyelid. 'And what do you want, mother?' she said turning to Anfisa. Her cod eyes gleamed with bureaucratic malice, the like of which you meet in every office, every waiting-room.

'My son, Vadim Gromov, Vadim Fyodorovich.'

'Look downstairs on the notice-board!'

'His name's not there.'

'Well, if it's not there that means he's not on it – it means he's not accepted, understand?'

'Yes.' Anfisa didn't budge.

'Well, is your son an invalid then? Why can't he come himself? Or is he still at kindergarten?'

'Don't take it too much to heart, dear,' said another girl, an insignificant looking little thing. 'If he didn't get in this time they'll take him next year.'

'We always have such an awful time with these mothers!' sighed the first. 'They don't know the meaning of discipline! They come rushing over here and there's nothing we can do for them.'

'Wait a moment, Alka', said the insignificant little one. 'Maybe he's on the supplementary list.' She bit her tongue, realising from the other's face that she'd said something she shouldn't have.

'Oh, is there a supplementary list?' asked Anfisa with beating heart.

'It's not confirmed yet,' said Alla. 'And why did you shoot your mouth off?' she said to the insignificant one.

'Please, my dears,' Anfisa Maximovna implored. 'Just let me take a little look.' She eventually persuaded them, and there with her own eyes, letter for letter, she saw the name 'Gromov, V. F.'

So now she could die in peace. Vadim would force his way in if necessary.

Anfisa went out, showering them with thanks and oblivious with joy. Her legs bore her along like a feather,

her plumpness and breathlessness quite forgotten. At the entrance to the institute there was a telephone box. She went in and dialled the number of the dean, Sergei Petrovich.

'Forgive me for bothering you, it's Anfisa Maximovna Gromova again – I came to see you, d'you remember?'

'Ah yes, I remember,' said Sergei Petrovich, somewhat doubtfully. 'What can I do for you now?'

'They've accepted Vadim.'

'Ah good, I'm so glad.'

'I just wanted to thank you. I'm really so grateful for . . . '

'For what? There's nothing to thank me for, my dear.'

Anfisa gripped the heavy receiver, warm with her breath, and said nothing.

'D'you hear?' said the dean sternly.

'Yes.'

'Remember now, you owe me nothing. Is that clear?'

'Yes.'

'But I'm very pleased for you, very pleased indeed. And greetings to your offspring. Come and see us some time. Sofia Vladimirovna and I will be delighted to see you.'

'Thank you.' Anfisa hung up. No, she'd never visit them again.

Her conversation with the dean had cast a slight shadow over her joy, but it was still alive. It was Vadim who finally killed it off.

'Congratulations to the student!' she said playfully when she got in.

Vadim raised his head indifferently: 'But I wasn't accepted. My name wasn't on the list. I looked.'

'But you're on the supplementary list. I saw it myself: Gromov, V. F.'

'And who asked you to go?' shouted Vadim. 'Won't you ever leave me in peace?'

'I'm your mother, Vadim! Every mother cares about her son!'

'But there's no need for you to care! It's a horrible fourth-rate little institute and I never wanted to go there in the first place! I just wanted to go out to work! God, however did I get myself into this?'

Anfisa Maximovna blinked rapidly.

'Going to start howling again, are you?' said Vadim spitefully. 'I'm sick to death of your film shows! I left once and I'll leave again, and this time it'll be for good, I'm warning you!'

So that was the end of her happiness . . .

It took her a long time to fall asleep that night, and she slept badly, with stupid, ridiculous dreams about bookshelves moving towards her and trying to crush her. She tried to escape them but they kept following her. She also dreamed of those knot-shaped pastries and Sofia Vladimirovna's hands, which reminded her of them. She tried to kiss these pastries, but Sofia Vladimirovna wouldn't let her, just laughed a little laugh and scattered raisins in the air. These dreams left her exhausted, and towards morning she had yet another dream: Fyodor returned from the dead, stood there menacingly before her and asked, 'What have you done with my son?' In this dream Fyodor was Vadim's father, and Anfisa was guilty of conceiving him with another man. She suffered and wept so much from this dream that she woke up, swimming in tears, her ears filled with a thin, mosquito-like buzzing, like a light-bulb just before it burns out. And her cheek was paralysed – it was quite numb. She rubbed it and that didn't help, she pinched it and she couldn't feel any pain. It was quite funny really – one of her cheeks was dead! But it passed.

[26]

That autumn Vadim started at the institute. He hated it from the start. When the students gathered for the first higher mathematics lecture in the large hall, with its two tiers of windows and its semi-circle of seats like an amphitheatre, Vadim looked around him with distaste – no, he most definitely didn't like it. He didn't know what he did want, but it certainly wasn't this. The lecture started. The professor, all dry and bristly, reminded Vadim of a cross between a Caspian roach and a toothbrush and evoked his immediate revulsion. He started off with a Latin saying, which he then translated into Russian. 'Showing off,' decided Vadim.

He didn't understand a single word of the lecture. The professor spoke smoothly and fluently in sentences of such length and complexity that the sense got completely lost in all the participles and adverbs, and you'd have forgotten the beginning by the time he reached the end. At first Vadim tried to take notes, but he soon got tired and gave up. Besides which he didn't know how to spell certain words, and he was afraid one of his neighbours might peer over his shoulder into his exercise book. He began to look round the auditorium instead: he greatly disliked what he saw here too, especially the enormous number of girls, and their great ugliness. Their presence annoyingly confirmed what he already knew – that this was a second-rate, provincial institute, where people went merely because there was less competition, and where no self-respecting lad would choose to go. The girls, many of whom wore glasses, took notes diligently and gazed up at the professor with beseeching eyes. Vadim was convinced they'd all come here to find a husband. What else would they be doing? A woman engineer would make a cat laugh. But Vadim didn't like the boys much either, especially the one with the mane of hair which he kept tossing back in a devil-may-care manner. And another, white as an albino, who looked as if he'd spent several years under the ground. These two were the nearest to Vadim, so he looked at them particularly carefully and with particular loathing. He was especially irritated by the attention with which they stared at the blackboard and frantically wrote down everything the professor said – most of it just empty words when it came down to it. These words knocked against Vadim's ears like peas in a rattle. He tried not to listen and to think his own thoughts, but he couldn't find anything good to think about. Vadim had long been convinced that he'd been given less than other people, done out of his rightful share of things. So now at the lecture, as he put his elbows on his narrow desk and rested his chin on his fist he didn't really think, he just went over in his mind all his resentments and took up arms against the world even more fiercely than before. He recalled his teacher's sardonic smile in the first class when he couldn't read the difficult word 'slipper' and everyone had laughed, and he didn't even know what 'slipper' meant. Later Olga Ivanovna had explained that a slipper was a kind of shoe. Why had the others laughed at him? None of them would have known what it was if they'd been asked. For a long time after this episode he refused to read aloud: this might have been the reason he never really learnt anything . . .

He recalled how the boys from his yard had come out looking so smart on Victory Day. Some of them even had fathers holding their hands, and the father of one of them had let his son put on all his medals. Vadim too found a medal at home, pinned it on and went out to the yard. And Petka Gavrilov said to him: 'But you never had a father . . . ' He remembered Svetka calling him a snivelling little husband, and he seethed with rage. No, they wouldn't make a fool of him any more! Then he thought of his mother with that complicated mixture of pain and suffocation which always accompanied his thoughts about her, his arguments with her and his entire life with her in the neat room wallpapered with the dreary green squares alternating with dreary green diamonds . . . And life in general was so dreary.

At that moment the professor had evidently made some sort of joke. Vadim didn't hear it of course, although he heard the students' laughter – ingratiating it sounded to him – and he saw with revulsion how the professor laughed with them, bearing his yellow teeth as he did so. This first lecture decided it for Vadim: the institute was loathsome to him, he had made a great mistake in coming here to please his mother. But he wouldn't be taken in again, he wasn't that stupid. He wasn't sure yet exactly what he would do, but one thing was clear: he had to prove something to someone . . .

[27]

When people asked Anfisa how things were she invariably replied: 'Thank God for everything!' Her son was settled at the institute and now she could rest. To me too she'd say, 'Thank God for everything!' But I didn't believe her: her eyes looked far too anxious. She must have been seriously ill even then, but she didn't yet give any sign of it. Her appearance had changed greatly for the worse though: she had put on weight and became breathless whenever she moved, as though she were crossing some boundary with every step she took. But what mainly alarmed me were the fits that periodically overcame her – fits of rage and despair when she screamed and beat her fists and scratched her face and hands, finding a desperate satisfaction in this wild loss of control. I persuaded her to go to a neuropathologist, and he found all the symptoms of hysteria and prescribed powders, drops, lotions and a diet. At first she took the powders and drops, but the bromide gave her a cold; so she stopped taking it and the cold passed (although she didn't again become more agitated). The less said about the diet and lotions the better. Our doctors seem to have little understanding of women's hard-working lives when they prescribe all these regimes and diets. What's the good of a diet when a woman's simply run off her feet? Anfisa worked one-and-a-half shifts, then there was the shopping and the housework to do, and all this at the expense of her sleep, of course. At her age she could have retired and lived on a pension, but that was out of the question – because of Vadim. But that didn't please Vadim particularly. He worked grudgingly, and frequently played truant. He got mainly twos in the first term and didn't get his grant renewed, and in response to his mother's reproaches he merely sulked and smoked. Anfisa bent over backwards to feed and clothe him. Vadim simply ignored her and didn't appreciate anything. 'It's like a bottomless pit,' Anfisa would say. 'I'm throwing myself away.'

What was going on? Was it all Vadim's fault? Certainly not. There are always two sides in any conflict, two versions of the truth. Certainly Vadim wasn't the only one of us to blame. Anfisa and I were to blame too. Especially me. I should have been more intelligent: unlike Anfisa I wasn't a victim of maternal love . . .

At times I barely recognised her. Before she'd been full of the joys of life and had loved jokes, music and books. She didn't read an enormous amount, but what she did read she always remembered perfectly, in the minutest detail (we who read a lot never remember things in such detail), and she often astonished me with the acuteness of her observations. For instance she noticed that both Nekhlyudov and Levin* were one and the same character, and said: 'Tolstoy must have been writing about himself.' She read the papers attentively too. She especially liked 'From the Hall of Justice', but she would glance at the political articles too. 'Cuba, where's that then?' she said, eagerly seeking out the little island, with my assistance, on Vadim's school globe. She saw animals, birds, trees, flowers. She rejoiced in the sun. Now it seemed to cast a shadow over everything for her. She stopped listening to the radio, almost stopped talking to people and was constantly rushing off somewhere with her strange, headlong, tilting gait. This haste was strikingly inconsistent with her slow, lumbering walk and her swollen legs.

Life started dogging her with petty misfortunes: she broke things, lost money, got short-changed in shops. She reacted violently, even melodramatically, to all this, rolling her eyes and tearing at her hair, her hands and legs trembling. And I'm sorry to say that I condemned her for these spectacles. I was sorry for her but I couldn't quite believe her grief was genuine – it was too clamorous. Then it seemed to me that real grief should be silent. I was wrong. Now I know better – everyone's grief is different.

Being very sensitive, Anfisa sensed my disapproval and withdrew into herself. She didn't visit me so often and was careful not to cry in front of me. We lost our old intimacy, our avid sociability. She refused my books now, saying: 'I haven't time, my life's a picture-book as it is.' That seemed false to me too. Occasionally we would quarrel, without the old scenes and the throwing of presents, but with a grim, cruel sadness. There were none

*The heroes in Tolstoy's *Resurrection* and *Anna Karenina*.

of the sweet and joyful reconciliations either. I felt at the time that I was totally right. What a cruel delusion! Lord save me from being right ever again! The person who is right is blind and deaf; the person who is right is a murderer.

From time to time she was attacked by a sort of slight, temporary paralysis: her finger would go numb, or her cheek, or she'd be suddenly unable to feel her heel and would start hopping along uncertainly. It always passed quickly, but nevertheless it worried me. Again I persuaded her to visit the doctor. She went, but returned disappointed: 'Same as before – nerves, hysteria, bromide drops. Doctors don't understand a thing. They say it's hysteria, I think it's just life. If you don't know life you just write out a prescription.'

That referred to me of course: Anfisa like to reproach me for not knowing life.

At that complicated time Vadim became almost an enemy: he barely acknowledged me, never visited me, and responded with a sneer to all my attempts to be sociable. Things at the institute weren't going well. He didn't like talking about it but his pride didn't allow him to lie. He admitted everything: bottom in maths, bottom in Russian . . .

'And I have to resit the exams, would you believe it! I couldn't care less whether I pass them or not!'

Once he said, 'You don't understand a thing, even though you're so old. University education, pah! What's the point? You went to university but you don't know about life.' They both kept referring to life. Maybe I really didn't know life, but it hurt me deeply nonetheless . . .

[28]

Vadim continued to go to the institute, intoxicated with his contempt for it. He loathed everything about the place: the gold memorial plaques recording the names of those who had studied there before (what they call learning, hah!), and the portraits of scientists in the corridors (including that of the senior mathematician with the yellow teeth who had given the first lecture and who afterwards took such enormous pleasure in giving him twos), and the wall newspapers filled with stories about students who broke the rules and students who fell behind with their work. Vadim was one of these laggers, not because he was stupid, mind, but because he was proud – although no one understood this, of course.

They positively roasted them at the institute, even in the hottest weather; the burning radiators would turn the place into a steam bath, and Vadim suffocated. He didn't attend most of the lectures, and usually went there only from two to three – as long as the monitors didn't notice. There were quite enough of these monitors though, what with the class leader, the Komsomol organiser and the trade union organiser. Vadim hated them all, apart from anything else because they were all women. He particularly disliked the trade union organiser, Lyuda Nikitina, with her milky plumpness, her fair hair and the gold earrings in her small clean ears. Whenever she tried to conduct an educational conversation with him she would blush a blotchy raspberry red and chew the end of her pencil with her fine little white teeth. Vadim was convinced that the conversations and the re-education were all a pack of lies, and that she was really in love with him. Vadim was very handsome and knew it, and this gave his relations with women a somewhat crude ruffian-like quality. True, he wasn't nearly so good-looking as he'd been as a child, when people would turn round in the street to stare at his big black eyes and splendid smile. But he couldn't remember himself as a child, so he couldn't make the comparison.

At one lecture in 'theormech' (theoretical mechanics) a fat, bespectacled, little student called Savelev, whom Vadim barely knew, sat down beside him. He went by the odd woman's name of Klavochka, and had an untidy fringe of hair falling almost into his spectacles. His greasy chest was covered with a shirt whose buttons were all torn off, and in one ear he wore an earring. He was drawing something diligently in his excercise book. Vadim glanced over his shoulder and he saw that it was of naked women. Vadim generally disliked this sort of drawing, but this seemed to be executed rather tastefully. They went out together after the lecture. 'What are you then, a painter?' Vadim asked. He had anticipated some sort of trite response, like: 'Yes, from the word "pain".' But instead Klavochka said, 'I'm not anything.' His round brown eyes blinked under their flashing spectacles.

'You like women?'

'I don't like anything. I merely exist.'

Vadim liked this. He too would like merely to exist, but couldn't manage it. He always seemed to be obliged to someone.

So they started going around together. They both cursed the theormech professor and theormech itself, which they saw absolutely no point in, since you never met with such abstractions in real life. Klavochka said that all science was irrelevant anyway, and to be an engineer the main thing was to have flair. Vadim liked this too. So he wasn't so bad after all with his negligent attitude to science – he did at least have flair, he could feel it in his chest. But he didn't yield quickly to sympathy: if he liked someone he would first of all suspect them of self-interest. So he began by asking Savelev with a teasing air: 'So why are you called Klavochka like a woman?'

'My brainy parents were first-generation intellectuals you see – they wanted a rare and beautiful name and they came up with Klavdii. They certainly did me a big favour! I took it very hard at first, and wanted to change it by deed poll – you know, put a notice in the paper saying Klavdii Savelev hereby changes his name to Genii Vetoshkin. But I thought better of it: it wasn't worth the candle . . . '

'I've always hated beautiful names too,' said Vadim, who also had a beautiful name. And all his grief against his mother stirred within him and welled up.

So Vadim and Klavdii soon struck up a friendship – not so much a friendship, more like the solidarity of outcasts. They were united by their mutual loathing of mathematics and their critical attitude to everything in general. They both despised the institute, science, good students, careerists and all the teachers and educators without exception. They just expressed it differently. Klavochka was cheerful about it, while Vadim was tragic. Klavochka was always fooling around: he'd imitate the professors and the Komsomol leaders, with their long speeches lashing out at laziness and slovenliness; he'd make faces behind the teachers' backs (teaching Klavochka was considered to be an onerous social duty): and he did it so light-heartedly. Vadim couldn't do that. He seethed inside when they tried to teach him. And he was always so envious of other people. These other people were always looming before him with their enviable sociability, their ability to engage and merge with others. Klavochka didn't envy anyone. He was a sybarite. 'I'd like to be on castors so I could just roll downhill,' he would say.

At the end of their year they were both bottom of the class. Expulsion was now seriously on the cards. But Klavochka wasn't downhearted: 'Remember what Khodja Nasreddin said when the shah ordered him to teach a donkey to read, "Something's bound to happen – one of us will kick the bucket, either the shah, or the donkey, or me. And meanwhile . . ."'

Meanwhile there was youth, there was Moscow with its L-shaped backstreets, its straight boulevards, its shop windows filled with expensive, inaccessible things. There were strong legs, perpetual pennilessness and vague hopes for what lay just round the corner. There were parties with people they barely knew, at which Klavochka skilfully playing on his teeth and never at a loss for words, was invariably the life and soul of the evening. And of course there was kissing in the backstreets, leaning briefly on soft shoulders, and rare, stunning meetings, hidden away in the mazes of communal flats, behind someone's door, behind someone's back – maybe that of a husband. Vadim didn't love any of these women, but at times he'd walk around feeling quite drunk from the experience.

The institute had receded into the background by now. Back there the jolly sociable student life went on as usual and they all prepared for exams, wrote cribs, crammed their appmaths and their theormech, sat for exams, resat them, gave talks, sang in the amateur choir, discussed class records and sports . . . What a fuss there was when a student took first place in some national high-diving contest! The kids would all be so pleased and proud, although they knew perfectly well that the champion had been in the first year for four years, and was desperately trying to earn enough marks to move up. Everyone knew this, but it didn't seem to bother them at all, it didn't touch their hearts as it did Vadim's. He had made a virtue of his inability to suffer from lying: it was a matter of honour for him, it put him above the rest, it meant he was more sensitive, more honest. It was just that somehow no one had noticed this . . .

Spring arrived with the smell of opening leaves, and warm hands clasped in the winding side streets. Of course neither Vadim nor Klavochka attended the spring session. Their hopes that someone would kick the bucket – either the shah, the donkey or Nasreddin himself – didn't materialise: no one kicked the bucket and both Vadim and Klavochka were up for expulsion. Klavochka, true to himself, refused to be downhearted: 'Who knows, it may be all for the best . . . To work at something all your life which you're not suited to is as bad as living with a woman who has bad breath.'

'But what *do* you like doing?' asked Vadim.

Klavochka thought a while, then said: 'What I'd really like to do is exploit someone's labour, but since that's impossible under present conditions, I shall have to go to the virgin lands.'

Bragging again! It was all very well for Klavochka to brag – he had no mother, just an elderly father, a retired teacher living on a pension out in the provinces somewhere, who barely even knew where his son was studying. Quite a different matter from Vadim. The very idea that he should tell his mother everything gave him cramp in the jaw. He'd do it as quickly as possible, as coarsely as possible, anything to get it over with. He went home and said: 'I've had it. I've danced to your tune long enough. I'm leaving the institute and going to the virgin lands!'

Anfisa Maximovna froze. She looked at him disbelievingly with shining grey eyes. 'You're joking, my son!'

'Why should I joke? Look, I've got my ticket in my pocket!'

Anfisa Maximovna slipped off her chair on to the floor and tried to clasp Vadim's legs. She was fat and ridiculous. Vadim shuddered with a moment of intense pity, then quickly got the better of it: 'Oh, don't put on another of your comic turns for God's sake – I can't take any more!'

Anfisa Maximovna lay there on the floor in a dead faint; she was a pale, almost green colour. Vadim ran out and rapped on Olga Ivanovna's door: 'Go and see her, do your comic turn together! I've had enough – I'm tired of playing your game!'

Olga Ivanovna got up in alarm, wrapping a shawl round her angular shoulders: 'What's the matter, Vadim?'

'I'm leaving the institute and I'm off to the virgin lands. Mother's fainted. It's all your fault, you taught her that . . . '

[29]

When Vadim had left for the virgin lands Anfisa Maximovna wilted, became limp and flabby. And worst of all, her work no longer excited her: the children's babble left her cold.

The idea of retiring on a pension gradually took shape in her mind: to live out the end of her days in freedom, sleep whenever she wanted to, take walks whenever she wanted to, read books whenever she wanted to.

'I've never had a moment for my own pleasure!' she said, plucking at her dress and flashing her eyes angrily. 'If I retire I'll be able to please myself for a change!'

I tried to talk her out of it: 'Don't do it, Anfisa Maximovna! You'll hate being without a job. I'm a year older than you, and an invalid too. I could retire but I go on working.'

'Don't compare me with you, you've had an easy life!'

'An easy life, eh? Well, I never . . . You know how my

life has been. Don't you think I've had enough grief?'

'But there's different kinds of grief. Yours was terrible but noble, without shame. Shameful grief ages you and wears you down. You've not known shameful grief.'

'Don't envy me, Anfisa Maximovna.'

'And you've had an education. If I retire I'll have time to catch up and get some education too!'

Well, what could I say to her? Let her retire, maybe it really would be the best thing for her.

[30]

So Anfisa Maximovna retired. They gave her a splendid send-off; the directress made a speech about the humble heroines of labour and they presented her with an expensive leaving gift – a gold-plated watch. Anfisa Maximovna wept: she was sorry to be leaving the children, sorry to be leaving her comrades, even sorry to be leaving the directress, although truth to tell she was rather a grumbler and much too punctilious.

The first few days passed quickly. It felt very strange to her not to have to get up early – she could sleep till midday if she wanted. Sleeping late had always seemed an outrage to her, as bad as stealing. Well, so what, she told herself; it was a well-earned rest. Now she could rest as much as she wanted.

But in fact she soon found she had nothing to do. Her own modest needs hardly took up any of her time: tea, buckwheat porridge, cabbage soup which lasted a few days, a small teapot, a small saucepan like the ones the children used in the nursery. And when she'd finished and washed up she'd be overcome with boredom. She'd pick up a book, but it seemed so dull and pointless – she wanted to read about life but all they ever wrote about was socialist emulation. She'd turn on the radio and that would be so dull too – she soon tired of popular songs, and classical music exhausted her. Sometimes the cat would come up, arching his back and rubbing himself against her. At least he was a living creature.

'Well then, little cat, you and I are all alone here now.' The cat purred. He was soft, but he too was dull company.

'Take lots of walks,' the doctor had said. 'Get out as much as you can.' So she went out for walks – she must keep busy, after all. She went back to her old nursery school and peered over the fence at the children playing, and she felt so sorry for them, as though they were her own children. There was a new teacher there now, a young woman reading a book and paying no attention to the children – and Misha Pantyukhov was crouching over a puddle and drinking the water. What was the girl thinking of? 'Misha! Come away from that puddle this minute!' Anfisa Maximovna shouted. Misha obeyed, then he recognised her and so did all the others.

'Anfisa Maximovna!' they shouted, running up to the fence and reaching out to her. The teacher dropped her book and hurried over to the fence. 'It's not allowed to talk to the children on the premises, citizen!'

Citizen indeed! So it had come to that, had it, being called citizen in her own nursery!

She didn't visit the nursery again after that. It would only have upset her.

She missed Vadim terribly. He wrote rarely, brief unloving letters. About himself he said little: he was well, he was working, things weren't too bad. One holiday he sent her a postal order. It wasn't much, but it was better than nothing; no words, just the money. She wept with joy, and sadness too. She felt so sorry for her son. He was living in some barracks poor boy, with the winds howling outside. She'd once seen a picture of the virgin lands and it was nothing but howling winds and endless barracks. But what worried her most was that he wouldn't find a wife out there on the steppes. There weren't many girls in that part of the world, and those there were were either lazy or shrewish. He'd bring her home and introduce her: 'Mama, meet my wife.' And his wife would giggle, crook her little finger and turn up her nose at honest hard work . . . Anfisa played out the whole scene in her mind. Her daughter-in-law would insult her and refuse to feed her: 'You're too old now, mother,' she'd say. 'You don't need to eat.'

Anfisa Maximovna, always so generous in the past, now became increasingly mean, and lived in constant fear that her pension wouldn't go far enough. She had developed a passion for sweet things, and ate them on the sly in her room so as not to have to share them with the others. If they saw her eating, Kapa would be sure to broadcast it all round the house: 'D'you know, Gromova's on a pension and she's eating cakes! Where can she get the money from?' Then they'd start to check and before she knew it they'd take away her pension – it does happen. Her free time was consumed in quarrels with Kapa. Kapa blamed her for Vadim: 'You've eaten up his future. You've an insatiable belly. You destroyed one person, and not content with that you started on another.' The old friendship with Olga Ivanovna had gone too. Anfisa had gone in to confide in her once, and Olga Ivanovna had thrust a book at her like some kind of medicine. That book of yours is about other people, my friend, Anfisa had said; give me something about me instead. But Olga Ivanovna had just pursed her lips and sniffed. She disdained tears. People were right when they called her stiff and proud. But what had she got to be proud about? The fact that she was still working and wasn't living on a pension? No, my dear, old age is old age – it'll get you in the end, however firm you stand. It may be a year sooner, it may be a year later, but in the end everyone has to retire on a pension.

Anfisa Maximovna started sleeping badly. She'd wake up in the middle of the night and lie there thinking. And there was always a terrible ringing in her ears.

[31]

Vadim had been in the virgin lands for two years now. He worked and he sulked and he still wanted desperately to prove something to someone, even though there was nothing to prove, and he turned out to be the most ordinary fellow in the world, even worse than other people in some ways. He lived in a hostel with Klavochka Savelev, and Klavochka too had lost his sparkle in Siberia; he grew a beard, his fringe became matted, his jokes fell flat, and he too, for all his free intellect, turned out to be the most ordinary fellow in the world. They just didn't have time to cut a dash now. The work was too gruelling. Vadim learnt to drive a truck. The technical equipment was crummy and there weren't enough spare parts. At busy times he didn't even manage to get to bed – it would be just one trip after another, day and night. On the steppes the wind howled and the sun burnt. In the winter snowstorms swept the ground and the snow would pile up treacherously high, so you couldn't see anything, even the road or the hostel.

Once Vadim drove out in a snowstorm and lost his way on the steppes. Then the motor went dead and he was stranded there with his truck. He tinkered around with the engine, but there wasn't a spark of life. So he hid in a corner of the cabin, wrapping himself up in all the bits of material he could find. The cold set in implacably and he grew afraid. He remembered stories about drivers freezing to death on the steppes. One man, they said, had crawled under his truck and propped it up with a jack, but the truck had collapsed on top of him and crushed his arm. He struggled and struggled, and shouted and shouted – and froze to death. Next morning they found his body with the arm gnawed to the bone: he'd tried to save himself by eating his own arm, but he couldn't bite through the bone. Vadim had always boasted that he cared nothing for life, but now, overcome with terror, he cursed his fate and howled with misery.

His comrades found him next morning and took him straight off to the hospital. It turned out he had frost-bitten toes, nothing more. But he had to stay in bed. The doctor complained that he was a lazy patient – he just didn't want to get better.

While Vadim was in hospital a nurse called Zhenya fell in love with him. She was an ill-favoured girl of about thirty, with bright eyes, a halo of hair and no figure to speak of. She gave him first-class treatment, washing and shaving him with eau-de-cologne, bringing him chocolates and vitamins. Vadim patronisingly allowed her to love him and look after him. Plenty more where she came from, he thought. He was secretly keeping himself for something else, although he wasn't too sure what. Something higher. As he had nothing better to do he read books, which Zhenya also brought him. He read inattentively, having decided in advance that everything in them was a pack of lies, although he liked books about spies, for they didn't have to be true. Once he got hold of a book with no beginning or end – they'd both been torn out, and there was no author or title either. He liked this book. A thief, a convict, went to rob a bishop, and the bishop gave him some candlesticks . . . and so on in this vein. Vadim was very taken with this book, and he gritted his teeth when he came to the last page and there was no end.

His friends came to visit him, lads from the lorry depot.

They slapped him on the back, roared with laughter at their own jokes, talked about spare parts and salaries – and he found it all extremely tedious. He considered himself above such petty concerns. He lay there listening to their conversation, with an expression on his face like Lord Byron. But unfortunately the lads didn't notice.

'You'd better get well and discharge yourself! Things have really hotted up back there!' they said.

Klavochka Savelev came to see him once, looking unrecognisably clean. His fringe was cut, he'd shaved off his beard and was wearing a sweater with a reindeer pattern. He didn't fool around. 'Well, my friend,' he said in embarrassment, 'I've got married.'

Vadim sniggered. He didn't ask who she was; he knew only too well. He asked only where he was going to live. With his wife, Klavochka said.

'Don't sign out of the hostel though,' said Vadim. 'It won't cost you anything. Leave us your bed.' Klavochka promised.

Vadim stayed in bed for a while longer, then went back to work. He lived alone in his room now, and Klavochka's bed was empty. Zhenya came twice a week – to wash, clean and cook for him. She'd stay the night too of course, and in the morning she'd leave, clinging to him with eyes like burdocks, just waiting for him to say: 'Let's get married.' But he wasn't falling for that. Klavochka now, he was a married man and led a quiet life – and what had become of him? He worked as a rate-fixer and his wife was a fat, mean, shrewish woman. Oh Klavochka, Klavochka, you've sold yourself short.

Vadim lived all alone with his hungry restless soul, forever analysing it and shaking it up, forever trying to discover where he'd gone wrong. Above all he was bored with himself. He no longer even found comfort in his cherished conviction that it was all a pack of lies. So what was left? He longed for something, but he didn't know what. Now for some reason he began to notice what in the past he'd contemptuously referred to as 'natural phenomena'. When he went to work in the morning he would look at the sky and the little pink barefoot clouds, or at the great circular steppe, combed with furrows by the plough, or at the rooks clamouring from their hollows in the earth, and he felt his heart keel over and capsize. Strangest of all was that he started thinking more and more about his mother, and the thought of her no longer suffocated him, but touched him. He missed her tears, her meekness, the melting way she called him 'my son'.

[32]

After Vadim had left Anfisa became gloomy and unsociable, and my ties to the communal family were somewhat weakened too. Oddly enough, the reason for this was partly the television. Panka Zykova had bought one on credit, and she was so proud of her new acquisition that she let anyone watch it who wanted to. So now the inhabitants of the flat spent almost every evening in front of the television with identical blue faces, their faces fixed on the flickering, slightly speckled screen. Even Kapa Gushchina, devout churchgoer that she was, succumbed to temptation. Anfisa didn't watch it every evening – it tired her eyes – and I preferred to pass the evenings with an old-fashioned book.

But one evening Panka Zykova said to me, 'Why don't you stay, Olga Ivanovna?' (With the purchase of the television she'd become kinder and more sociable). What could I do? I was too old for television, of course. And the older I got the more tenderly and jealously I loved my work. I was afraid I'd have to leave it soon – they'd abolish the job or make me retire.

What a marvel it is to work with children! They poured around me like a flowing stream. They were always changing – some left, others arrived, and that had its own sad charm.

It terrified me to think what might have become of me had I happened to be a clerk, say, in some office. I would have died.

Time passed, and our children at the House of the Child were better fed and clothed now, more handsome and intelligent. I had learnt how to pick out the gifted ones, simply from the expression in their eyes. I know a teacher isn't supposed to make distinctions and have favourites, but I did. I especially loved two little girls, a dark one and a fair one, Anya Lozhkina and Manya Vetkina. Anya was straight and tall for her age, with a face of porcelain darkness and such black eyes that they gleamed with blue. 'Anya Lozhkina has dark black eyes!' the other children would say. Anya was musical and had an excellent ear, but she was morbidly shy. Whenever I asked her to sing she would bury her face in my lap and from there she would sing a tune in her utterly true, delicate little voice. Manya Vetkina, on the other hand, was sharp and talkative; she had a low voice – a little childish bass. She had a tiny body on thin spidery legs, a large, fair, curly head, huge grey eyes and a mischievous smile. Manya could talk non-stop for a whole hour, and so intelligently too, so reasonably and clearly that everyone would be amazed. She could repeat almost verbatim a book she'd read the day before. Her one great weakness was her inability to recognise poetry and she would recite it as prose. When I managed to tear Anya Lozhkina away from my stomach, she and Manya Vetkina would sing a duet – a piccolo and a 'cello.

More and more people came to us now wanting to adopt a child – childless couples, or single women desperate to be mothers. Once a single man came. We would arrange times at which the future parents would choose themselves a son or daughter. What a cruel business it was, like a bride-show! The rules stipulated that the children mustn't be told they were being inspected and 'chosen'. But as fate would have it, they always did know. They even discussed in advance who would be picked. They considered it a tremendous stroke of luck to be chosen. They knew that people preferred the beautiful, strong, curly-haired ones, and Manya Vetkina was convinced they'd choose her: 'They all want the ones with curly hair.'

'What about your legs?'

Her legs were indeed very thin.

At the inspections in the music hall the children were all so modest, so meek, pleading with their every movement, their eyes, their arms, their backs: 'Take me, take me!' they seemed to say. And people chose the best, and took them away. One day Manya Vetkina was chosen. The day they took her away was one of the saddest in my life. I know I should have been happy for her. She was adopted by a woman who had just lost a daughter. She had a sensitive face and the same grey eyes as Manya's. By the time they left, Manya was calling her Mama . . .

*　　*

One day I got home from work to find Ada Efimovna standing by the door with a door-key in her hand and an anxious look on her face.

'Oh Olga Ivanovna, I'm so glad you're back. I've been trying to open the door, but it won't go. You know how hopeless I am at technical things. I keep ringing and ringing and there's no answer.'

'Is anyone in?'

'Anfisa Maximovna. She was in when I went out anyway. You try with your key.' I tried: the door was locked on the chain. I rang once, twice, three times. No one came.

Ada was pale, and I too was feeling very apprehensive by now. 'I know something's happened,' she said. 'I just know it.'

'She might be asleep,' I hazarded.

'No one sleeps like that, least of all her. She's such a light sleeper, she's always complaining of it.'

'Shall we call the janitor then?'

The janitor wasn't in his usual place, there was just an axe there. We stood outside in the courtyard. The house was being repaired and was covered in scaffolding. The window into the Gromovs' room was wide open. 'I'll climb up and open the door from inside,' said Ada.

'However will you climb in? It's on the third floor . . .'

'Up the scaffolding,' said Ada.

She began clambering up, agile as a monkey, her skirt billowing out around her like a bell. Down below some little boys shouted: 'Look at the old woman climbing!' It was like a bad dream. When she reached the third floor she waved to me and disappeared through the open window. I went up the stairs – the lift had broken down again – and rang the bell. No reply. Then suddenly there was a terrible noise in the corridor and Ada came rushing to the door shouting: 'My God, she's dead, she's dead!'

'Let me in!' I said.

Ada, shrieking, fumbled with the chain. 'What a nightmare! And now this chain.'

She eventually let me in and we both rushed to Anfisa's room. She was lying face down on the floor, her legs twisted clumsily inwards. I tried to lift up her face, but she was so heavy and awkward it was quite beyond my strength. She seemed to me to be alive and breathing though. 'Ada, ring at once for the emergency service!' I said.

'I'm going, I'm going!'

'Don't you understand, someone's dying here!' Ada shouted down the telephone. 'Stop bothering me for details!'

I went on trying to lift Anfisa, as though her life depended on it. I managed somehow to turn her on her side. But she immediately slumped again with her face to the floor. A gurgling sound came from her throat: so she was still alive.

The emergency service soon arrived. 'Stroke,' said the doctor. They loaded Anfisa onto a stretcher, carried her out and drove her away. I ran off to send a telegram to Vadim.

The flat grew quiet. That evening Kapa came in to see me. 'Olga Ivanovna, I've done my christian duty and tidied up Anfisa's room. She was a person too, after all.'

'You mustn't say "was", Kapitolina Vasilevna. She's still alive, you know.'

'Alive, but sure to die. The finger of God has pointed . . . She'd swelled up like yeast. I said to her once: "Why are you getting so fat?" She didn't like that. I knew it would end like this.' Kapa was being severe, but she was shaken and this made her attribute everything to herself. I offered her tea and she didn't refuse, although there was nothing to go with it.

'You'd never have a stroke, Olga Ivanovna, you've never been fond of sweet things, that's why you're so thin. I may well have one though, on account of my weight. It's easy on the eye but hard on the heart.'

After tea she said: 'Olga Ivanovna, let me sit here with you this evening. My room's next to Anfisa's and it scares me to go back there – makes me think of my own death.'

'Do sit here, I'd be delighted.' So Kapa spent the evening with me, and talked and talked. She pitied Anfisa and reproached herself: 'It's a sin on my conscience. I led the dear departed one into temptation. I should have kept quiet, but I had to argue with her instead. As if the devil had got hold of my tongue.' She stubbornly referred to the sick woman as the departed one, and I stopped contradicting her after a while. Somewhere far away Anfisa was lying inaccessible to us, without feelings, without speech. The darkness between us was so dense it differed little from death.

That evening Kapa recounted to me the entire story of her life. She was born in a village near Sergievsky Posad, now Zagorsk, and from her earliest years she had loved going to church. At Troitso-Sergii the cathedrals were just beautiful, one lovelier than the next, like being in heaven. Blue cupolas, gold stars, and as for the interiors . . . She described the church service at great length, trying to break through her own inert speech patterns to make me see it all: the yellow flame of the candles, the blue smoke from the incense, the angelic singing. She got angry with herself for not doing it justice, sighing and repeating with a prayerful sigh: 'Tender emotions are heaven's reward.'

Then she told me about her life: 'I got married against my will. I was married very young to an old man. Ugh! he was horrible, all bristly, with hairs growing out of his nose. He tried to force me to love him, but I was too young to know what love meant. But then I gave birth to a son, pretty as a picture, the very image of a cherub, like in the icon paintings. I loved him more than anything, I just idolised him – and of course it's a sin to idolise anyone. So God punished me. Kolenka was just three when he died. Caught scarlatina and choked to death. I carried him and rocked him and prayed that he should live. But he closed his eyes, put his little arms round my neck, gave one last sob and died.'

Kapa was silent for a while, then cleared her throat and went on in a different tone: 'Well, there you are, I didn't have any more children after that. My husband died shortly after Kolenka, and no sooner had I buried the old man than they married me off to another one. This one wasn't old but he was ugly as sin. He wasn't such a bad person though. And he was big, you wouldn't rob him on the highway, as they say. But he had this crooked mouth – his cheek had been slashed by a sabre and he always looked as though he was baring his teeth. All this was just after the civil war. It was the beginning of a new life for everyone else, but for me the old life went on as before. Our village was poor as could be. Father and mother had a brood of little children, all of them needing to be fed. What could I do, with all those mouths to feed? I got married to the man with the lopsided mouth. I got used to him – he turned out to be an honest enough fellow, not first-class but passable. He didn't smoke, didn't drink, didn't chase other women – he was all right, I've seen worse. He was killed during the collectivisation. He was helping to get the state farms going and some kulak took a shot at him. I howled then like you wouldn't believe. I was good at howling then, a real artist, the best in the village. Then my aunty Anisya said to me: "Kapa, do you want to go to Moscow?" I didn't understand anything then, little fool that I was – I hadn't even seen a tram. And I said: "Yes I do." So she took me to Moscow and set me up as a maid – or a cleaner it would be called now. Well everyone knows what it's like to be a cleaner – no disgrace, but not exactly an honour either. It wasn't bad, I survived. But then I fell desperately in love with someone who was married. I knew it was a sin to love a married man, but I loved him all the same. It was such a love that if you read about it in a book you wouldn't believe it. I loved him and went on living as a servant. But I thought he'd be ashamed of me, so I got a job in a factory. They gave me a place in a hostel. My girl friends felt sorry for me being so much in love, and they'd draw the curtains round their beds and not complain when the married man spent the night with me. So I lived in sin for some years, like a pig in muck, but then one day this married man's wife came to the hostel and tore my hair out. We fought and created a scandal, and the superintendent got to hear of it and they threw me out of the hostel. I had nowhere to go then, so I became a servant again, this time looking after a little girl, who I doted on. Then the married man left me. I loved looking after that little girl, but when it was time for her to go to school my employers said to me: "Goodbye and thanks, we don't need you any more." How could they? I couldn't believe it! I'd brought her up like my own child – and now they didn't need me any more! I started such a howling I got soaked through . . . But in the end I got myself a job as a night watch. They gave me this room here, and it was a good job – it left me lots of time for my soul. You just had to keep your eyes open and not fall asleep. I'd sit there in my thick sheepskin coat counting the stars, and it was then I started thinking about God – it's easier to think at night than during the day. God must surely have abandoned me for my sins by now, I thought. You're lying, said the twinkling stars, God is kind, he's a father to everyone. So I went to a priest to talk things over and he said: "God understands everything, he forgives all our sins, just pray." So I started praying and going to church, and now that I've retired I can say I never miss a service. The Soviet government gives me a pension, thank God. I've nothing against our government, they certainly care for us ordinary people. I just wonder why they closed down all the churches. There was a church in our village and it's a warehouse now. The church gives people such happiness, such beauty . . . I shall pray for Anfisa, I've sinned greatly against her. The Lord forgives everything, as long as you pray. I shall light a fifty kopeck candle for Anfisa – I don't grudge her the money . . . '

Kapa was silent for a while, then cleared her throat again and asked: 'Would you mind if I stayed the night here with you, Olga Ivanovna? I've got myself into a terrible state now. I'm scared to sleep on my own in case the dead come back to haunt me.'

'Do sleep here, Kapitolina Vasilevna. Take the bed, I'll sleep on the floor.'

'How could I let you sleep on the floor in your own

room? I have a folding bed of my own – thank God I'm not a beggar!'

Kapa brought it in, we made it up and went to bed. My room was so narrow that we had to jam her folding bed up against my bed. Kapa tossed and turned for a long time, with much squeaking and clanking, then said: 'Life is a wicked thing.' I didn't reply. 'Are you asleep, Olga Ivanovna?'

'No, I'm not asleep.'

'So you think there's no God?'

'That's right, I think there's no God.'

'Well, what about that falling thing then?'

'What falling thing?'

'The lamp. Listen to what happened to me. I was going to light a candle to Nikolai the Blessed, a large one, for one ruble. And suddenly I was seized with greed and I took a smaller one for fifty kopecks. I lit it and I thought: It's all one to a blessed saint, I'm just a poor woman. And what d'you think? That very same evening I was sitting in my room knitting a sock when the lamp over my head exploded and fell to the floor, and the broken pieces of lampshade fell straight onto my head. God saw that I'd begrudged Him the money for a candle, so He punished me. And that lampshade cost me more than a ruble, it cost a whole two rubles fifty. And then you say there's no God . . . '

'Go to sleep, Kapitolina Vasilevna, I'm not saying anything. Sleep well.'

She turned over again, grew quiet and fell asleep. I didn't fall asleep until morning.

[33]

Vadim returned a few days later, looking black as could be and a bit withered, and he went straight off to the hospital. Anfisa didn't recognise him. She lay there in a ward of ten people with shaven head and vacant gaze. All around her the other patients were groaning and wheezing and complaining. Anfisa just lay there in silence, her eyes glazed and lacklustre.

Vadim stayed in the hospital for days on end. He kept the doctors on their feet with his questions. 'What can we do?' they'd say to him. 'The whole of her right side's paralysed, including the speech centres.'

'Will she get better? Will she walk? Vadim interrogated the doctors as though they were careless servants.

They gave him vague answers, mainly in the negative: 'We don't know yet. There's been grave damage but maybe some functions will gradually be restored. The organism is basically sound . . . The heart's functioning quite well.'

* *

They soon got used to him at the hospital. He would go there every day, put flowers on the bedside table and sit down beside her on a rickety chair. He would sit like that for hours at a time, squeezing his knees with his large swarthy hands. On his left wrist was a watch; the hands moved quickly, but he didn't notice the time passing as he looked into her face, distorted by illness. One eye was open but vacant, the other was screwed up, as though winking.

'Mama!' he would call from time to time. 'Mama, can you hear me?'

His mother looked comically at him, as though saying, 'Have you got what you wanted?'

When they brought her food, Vadim would take the spoon and try to feed her. It wasn't clear whether she swallowed or not: at times there'd be a gurgling sound in her throat and a sort of swallowing shudder would pass down her neck. Liquids would pour out of her insensible lips and stain the pillowcase. Vadim would raise her heavy bristling head, tuck a towel under it and again lift the spoon to her leaden lips.

He threw himself headlong into caring for his mother. He did it fiercely and selflessly – he not only fed her and washed her, he did all sorts of other things too, the dirty and disgusting things that men usually disdain. Vadim didn't disdain anything, he did everything, with a dark, inscrutable, angry face.

When Anfisa Maximovna grew worse he got permission to spend his nights in the ward. The women who were convalescing would grumble: 'Why is there a man in the ward?' The paralysed ones didn't care. Vadim sat there like a statue, obediently turning away whenever they asked him to, astonished that this should matter. Hardest of all was when he caught someone whispering: 'That's the son! If only every mother had a son like him!' Then he would groan inside. With the doctors he was obdurate and demanding, infuriating them with his sardonic comments, not concealing the fact that he thought them all blockheads and ignoramuses, and eating their bread without paying for it. They treated him with affable hostility.

'We're not gods, don't you understand!' a young intern with a pink cheerful face said to him. 'We're doing everything we possibly can, I assure you, but it's a practically untreatable case. And if you add her age and weight . . . Every life has its limit.'

Vadim very nearly hit him. He was struggling for his mother's life, he didn't want to know about limits. He wanted her to live, he wanted her to say 'my son' to him just once more.

He would spend his days and nights in the ward hospital, snatching the occasional bite to eat in the neighbouring snackbar. Sitting at night on the squeaking chair, his head would loll and he would fall asleep. His eyes grew hollow, his nose grew sharp and rapacious and a terrible haunted look appeared in his eyes.

He didn't let any visitors in to see his mother: 'There's nothing for you to do here!' So he turned away Kapa, who appeared with a little bottle of holy water, and Ada Efimovna, who brought a box of chocolates. The box he rejected with a contemptuous 'Oh really!' For Olga Ivanovna, however, he made an exception: he sometimes allowed her to stand at the doorway to the ward. 'Seen enough?' he'd say. 'Satisfied?' Then he'd drive her out too.

[34]

Once I decided to have it out with Vadim and lay in wait for him in the corridor. He was carrying a bedpan and his face looked so angry, adult and unfamiliar that I involuntarily addressed him in the formal manner: 'Wait a moment, Vadim, talk to me. Why won't you let me in to see Anfisa Maximovna?'

'Because she doesn't need you!' he spat. 'You don't give a damn about her!'

'I won't argue with you. You know quite well that's not true. But don't you see, you can't just shut yourself off from other people like this. I have a boundless respect for what you're doing for her . . .'

'You can keep your boundless respect to yourself. If I do something it's not because I want your respect.'

'But just let me help you in some way.'

'Why should I? Why do you come here?'

'You're a strange person. I come because I love her and pity her and want to help.'

'That's just a pack of lies!'

I shuddered when I heard the adult word 'lies', instead of his old childish 'they're making it all up.'

'I am not lying! I'm sorry for her and sorry for you. You've got so much anger inside you!'

'It's just a pack of lies!' repeated Vadim in a frenzy. 'You say you pity her, but would you watch over her for days and nights on end like I do? Clean her, go through what I go through? If you'd do all that, then fine, stay here instead of me!' And he laughed. The nurse wiping the floor looked at him in horror.

'I can't do that, I have a job!'

'There you are, a job! So all that about your love and pity for her is just a pack of lies! If you really love and pity someone you don't care about anything else – work, house, family or friends. Would you give up your job for her? No! So there's nothing to talk about!'

He turned and walked into the ward.

[35]

He spent that night dozing as usual on the chair beside Anfisa Maximovna's bed. She lay there before him like a mountain, breathing with agonising difficulty, and he dreamt that his father Fyodor came, took him in his arms, kissed him and threw him up in the air. There were red hairs on his father's arms. Vadim passionately loved those hairs, those arms. Something had stood betwen his mother and father, and now Vadim was tearing that something apart and demolishing it. There was a loud cracking noise, something collapsed under him and he almost fell off his chair.

He awoke and again listened to his mother's breathing – hoarse, catching at every breath. And again he saw his father's arms, his father's arms . . .

* *

After about two months Anfisa Maximovna became a little better. She could open both eyes, her ironic squint disappeared and she began to swallow and eat. Vadim was happy. He lifted her up and surrounded her with pillows. She was pale and thin and totally unrecognisable, her shaven head now overgrown with a short grey bristle. But now her eyes were alert and wet with a sentient tear. One arm was still paralysed, but the other, thin and covered with injection marks, went up to her head, tried to tidy her hair and found none there. Her eyes looked bewildered. She even tried to speak, but no words came, and from her lips issued a series of stuttering, disconnected sounds – 'ti-ti-ti!', or 'kara-kara-kara!' She clearly wanted to tell him something, and he tried desperately to understand, put his ear to her lips and beseeched her: 'Tell me, Mother, tell me.' But it was just the same 'ti-ti-ti-kara-kara-kara!' as before, or the other way round: 'kara-kara-kara-ti-ti-ti!' over and over again.

When the doctors realised that the patient's condition had stabilised and there was nothing more to expect, they decided to discharge her. The chief doctor himself had a talk with Vadim.

'You're a young man, of course, we realise it would be hard for you to take on such a burden. But you must understand we can't keep chronic cases here. We need every bed we've got – you can see they're lying in the corridors as it is. Now where d'you work?'

'Nowhere at present. I've just been out to the virgin lands.'

'Well, you can make arrangements for her to go into a home for chronic invalids. They'll meet you half-way if you've worked in the virgin lands. You can get all the necessary information here.'

'It's all right thanks. I don't need any help. I'll be able to keep my mother somehow.'

'As you wish,' said the chief doctor. This young man commanded his grudging respect. 'We'll discharge her on Tuesday.'

* *

On Tuesday Vadim took Anfisa Maximovna home. She was pleased as a child and babbled her 'kara-ti-ti-kara!' Vadim gazed gloomily and affectionately at her, tucked in her blankets and put an alarm-clock by her ear. 'Tick-tock!' he said.

The flat discussed every conceivable aspect of Anfisa Maximovna's return, and heated gossip was again exchanged in the kitchen.

'He's a young man,' said Kapa. 'He'll want to get married. Wherever will he bring his wife if there's a body lying there in the room?'

'How can you think such things!' chirped Ada Efimovna. 'What would you say if something like that had happened to you?'

'I'd say God had laid me low and I'd take to my bed. Why burden another person? Better to get it over with and die, I say. Death's the same whether it happens in hospital or at home.'

Then Panka, who didn't usually take part in these conversations, unexpectedly voiced her opinion: 'We all have to die – you have to die, I have to die.'

It wasn't quite clear what she meant by this. But she seemed to be agreeing with Kapa.

'Why are you all being so critical?' said Olga Ivanovna. 'She's a sick woman and she's been brought home – that's all there is to it.'

'An invalid's an invalid, but we have to know what's what all the same,' said Panka.

[36]

I bought a few treats one day – apples, chocolates, biscuits – and knocked at the Gromovs' door. 'Come in,' said Vadim.

Anfisa Maximovna was lying in her wide, neatly made-up bed: it looked as though a woman's hands had made this bed, with the stitched blanket-cover, the magnificently plumped-up pillows and the smart satin quilt. On the pillows was a pale thin face, strangely altered by its grey crewcut: Anfisa, always so feminine, now looked like an old man. In the depths of her face swam two huge grey eyes. She recognised me, brightened up and started speaking, eagerly and rapidly: 'kara-kara-ti-ti-kara! Ti-ti-ti-kara-kara-kara! Kara-ti-ti-kara!'

In this stream of sounds there was a certain mad fluency, rhythm and expressiveness.

'Very interesting,' said Vadim. He was sitting at the table with his back half turned to us. Anfisa Maximovna looked indignantly at him ('My God, she understands everything!' I thought), and again started babbling the same sounds, but in a different order and in a different tone of voice: 'Kara-kara-kara-ti-ti-kara-kara!'

She seemed to me to be speaking quite intelligently but in a different language. I put the biscuits and sweets on the bedside table (elegantly covered with a white napkin) and she nodded at me and started up again in her own language. This time it was easy to understand: she was thanking me.

'That'll do now,' said Vadim, going up to the bed. 'You've seen her, that's enough. It's time for us to sleep now, isn't it mother?'

He stroked her grey bristly head. She threw him a pleading, tender, sidelong look and I left.

[37]

Days, weeks, months passed and Anfisa Maximovna's condition remained the same. Vadim looked after her as before. He was exhausted, worked off his feet by all the laundry. He would change sheets, wash them and put on clean ones, then do it again – and again and again . . .

He would spend whole days on end washing and boiling sheets. His gloomy figure was constantly to be seen bending over the kitchen sink. He rejected all offers of help.

'Let me do some washing Vadim,' pleaded Kapa. 'I don't mind, I'm used to it.'

'It's all right, I can do it,' Vadim replied.

He put a row of fishing-lines over the stove and hung up underwear right there in the kitchen, and even fierce Panka didn't dare object. He also cooked, clumsily and proudly, rejecting all offers of help. Having cooked dinner he would go and feed Anfisa from a spoon. He would feed her like an angry nursemaid feeding a recalcitrant child: 'Come on, eat up, open your mouth!'

Afterwards he'd have his own dinner, indifferently gulping down the cold tasteless remains of his mother's meal. Then he'd wash up the dishes and do the laundry all over again.

He soon got used to his life, and forgot there'd ever been any other. He had the money he'd earned in Siberia to be going on with, and he didn't think about the future. 'Either the shah . . .', as Klavochka used to say.

Sometimes he got angry with his mother and berated her. This was when it seemed to him that she was deliberately refusing to speak. He tried to teach her to speak: 'Now then mother, stop being stupid, let's get to work. Open your mouth and say "Ah!" Understand? "Ah!"'

'Kara-kara-ti-ti-kara!' answered Anfisa Maximovna.

'Stop jabbering,' said Vadim crossly. 'Say "Ah!"'

She tried hard, mooing, bellowing and shaking her head, but it was no good.

'You're being silly! I'm doing my best for you – look, I'm trying to teach you to speak, I know you can say everything and ask for everything. If you want tea you ask for it, and if you want something else you ask for that too. Now you're just acting like a dumb beast. Are you going to learn or aren't you?'

It was no good. Vadim even made an appointment with a speech therapist, but the man had nothing helpful to suggest, spoke of inhibition of the nervous centres and of curing the stammer through hypnosis. Then he asked how old the patient was and when Vadim told him he had nothing more to say.

After that Vadim decided to teach his mother grammar rather than speech. He bought a tattered ABC. 'Look, here's "A", and here's "M" – there, I've made "Mama". "Mama", understand? That's you!'

He poked her in the chest. She jabbered, nodded and poked herself in the chest with her good arm.

'Bravo! You understood! Now you make the word "mama"!' He took her hand in his and tried to make her cold limp fingers grasp the pencil. 'There you are!'

But it was no good. And the harder he tried the worse it went. Anfisa Maximovna nodded, agreed and understood, but she simply couldn't make words out of the letters. She got angry and cried; her face didn't wrinkle, but her eyes filled with pain and great transparent tears rolled down her cheeks. This silent weeping shook Vadim badly.

'You've got me by the throat again, damn it! Why d'you torment me like this? I'm doing it all for you, you poor numbskull! D'you want me to cry too? Look what you've made me do!' And he would burst into tears, howling and choking and gulping.

When it became clear that she wouldn't be able to read, Vadim abandoned the alphabet. But he didn't give up on her. He had to break through the wall between him and his mother, and establish some sort of communication with her. He had to do this, he didn't know why, it was just mortally necessary for him to do so. He took some coloured crayons and drew for her, like a child 'That's the sun, and it's red. And there's a leaf, and that's green. Understand? Now you take a red crayon. Not green, red. You don't know red! I'm telling you in plain Russian: red! That's good, well done . . . '

Vadim's praise gave his mother great joy and she blossomed under it. He worked patiently with her like a trainer, and in three months he had taught her to distinguish and pick up the red, the green and the blue crayons.

But eventually Vadim's money ran out and he had to find a job. He hated the idea of being a taxi driver, although it did pay well. A taxi driver's life meant always travelling from place to place, and he had to be as close to home as possible. Finally, thanks to the janitor's influence, he managed to get a job cleaning shoes and selling laces at a kiosk on the neighbouring street corner.

The kiosk was made of glass and Vadim used to sit there like an exhibit. Every two or three hours he would close it up and go home, feed his mother and change her sheets. Then he'd go back to his corner kiosk. He detested the work. Whenever he gave a customer some laces he'd screw up his eyes, grimace and deliberately choose the tattiest pair, and if they asked him for black he'd give them brown as though by mistake. He cleaned shoes conscientiously though, with a flourish of his worn velvet cloth. He rejected tips indignantly: once he threw a half-kopeck piece back at a customer, who promptly took offence and called a militiaman. The militiaman listened to both sides and decided in Vadim's favour.

'He's not to blame, citizen, it's you who've insulted a soviet person by giving him such a small tip. You should have given him at least fifty kopecks.'

Then some pensioners lodged a complaint against Vadim. They complained that he was almost never at his post and they often couldn't get their shoes cleaned when they wanted to. So after that he had to keep strictly to his hours, and run home only during the lunch hour. He didn't enter into any explanations about this.

One day Vadim was cleaning someone's shoes – solid, black, welted shoes – and raising his eyes he saw sitting before him, with his feet on the bench, none other than the former dean, Sergei Petrovich Navolochkin. Vadim almost died of humiliation. Strangely enough Sergei Petrovich remembered him.

'Fancy meeting you again, Gromov!'

Vadim said nothing, diligently polishing his shoes.

'Well, this is a fine business you've got here! I remember you never did like maths. I see you've found yourself a job without maths, eh?' The dean's heavy brows turned down into his eyes as bellicosely as ever. From below, his foreshortened face looked full of malicious glee.

'Why are you making fun of me?' said Vadim.

'What d'you mean? I wouldn't dream of doing such a thing! How's your mother?'

'She's ill,' replied Vadim curtly.

'Nothing serious, I trust?' Vadim shook his head. 'Well, send her my regards. And tell her that her old pupil Lucy is now at school and in the second class.'

Vadim finished the shoes. Sergei Petrovich got up, paid him with exactly the right money, adjusted his scarf and reached for his hat.

'Well, look after yourself. If you don't like your new job and ever feel like returning to the institute come and see me and we'll talk about it. Only no fooling around this time, eh?'

Vadim nodded. The institute, studying – it all seemed like another planet now.

* *

During the day he worked, but during the evenings and nights he washed. Anfisa Maximovna lay there in the same condition. She still said 'kara-kara-ti-ti-kara!' in various different ways, but her voice was quieter now and she was less lively.

One day he returned from work to find her lying on the floor near the door, clasping a chair. She had evidently tried to get out of the room and go somewhere, had gripped the chair, but hadn't managed to get up and had fallen. After this he started tying her to the bed and locking her in the room when he went out to work.

[38]

I was washing in the kitchen one day and heard noises from the Gromovs' room. Someone was groaning, weeping, almost howling in there. I knocked on the door.

'Anfisa Maximovna, it's me, can I come in?'

The sounds intensified. I pushed the door – it was locked. I looked for the key in all the places it was usually kept. The sounds became deeper, hoarser, then abated. Maybe she was dead!

I rushed downstairs to the janitor and begged him to break down the door.

'There's a sick woman locked up alone in there. She may be dead already . . . '

'I'm not allowed to force open a private dwelling – it's forbidden by the constitution.'

'Forget the constitution, there's a sick woman in there and we have to get to her!'

'But where's her son? At work? But that's just round the corner. You go and fetch her son.'

I rushed over to Vadim's kiosk. There was no sign of him there. 'He's gone to the depot,' said the militiaman. By now Anfisa could well be dead.

I dragged myself back to the janitor: 'Her son's not there, if you don't break down that door immediately I'll have you charged under article one-hundred-and forty six!'

I hadn't the slightest idea what this article was, but it did the trick. He came to break down the door, annoyed at being torn away from his work.

The door burst open with a groan. Anfisa Maximovna was lying there unconscious, her head lolling forward. I didn't immediately realise that she'd been tied up.

'That beast!' said Kapa, all curiosity. 'Tied up his mother like a goat out to graze!'

Anfisa was alive but unconscious, her good eye slightly open and gleaming dully. Then the doctor gave her an injection and revived her, and she started breathing hoarsely. She looked half dead. What had happened to her? What had she been so afraid of? She looked in horror out of the window. There had been something there. I sat by her bed. Time passed, it grew dark outside the window, she fell asleep.

Later that evening Vadim returned. Seeing the door broken down and me sitting by the bed he exploded with rage, moving towards me with lowered head and menacing fists: 'Who gave you the right to do that? I shan't leave it at this, you know! You'll have to answer for what you've done!'

I wasn't afraid. I'm never afraid of elemental disasters – thunderstorms, bombing raids or angry men.

'You had no right to lock her in and tie her up like an animal. Why did you do it? Just because you wouldn't accept help from anyone else!'

'Shut up!' shouted Vadim. 'A fat lot you understand, you loathsome woman!'

I calmly went back to my own room. Heavy footsteps approached my door, and Vadim opened it a crack and shouted: 'I forbid you to come into our room! D'you hear?'

'You're an idiot!' I said.

I wasn't so clever either.

From that day on Vadim stopped saying hello to me. They repaired the broken door and replaced the lock. Vadim would lock the door as before when he went out, but Kapa managed to spy out where he hid the key. Sometimes in his absence I would slip into the room like a thief, and Anfisa Maximovna would be lying there, quiet and old, her hair longer now, and stuck flat to the pillow. From time to time she would mutter: 'Kara-kara-ti-ti-kara!', but without her former animation. She was indifferent to guests. Her eyes were filled with fear, and she would look with horror out of the window, stretching out her arms as though to ward off some evil lurking outside. I would sit beside her for a while, then tiptoe out. She would accompany me with her eyes. Then I would lock the door again.

Worst of all was when Vadim started coming home drunk. Wild noises would be heard behind the door as he moved furniture around and laughed. Sometimes he would cry, howling and yelping like a dog. Once he brought a woman home with him.

Is there any limit to human suffering? I realised that Anfisa Maximovna was dying but I no longer wanted her to live: if only she'd die, I thought. We all think that when a terminally ill person is dying, having exhausted themselves and others in the process, and we justify ourselves by saying we want an end to their sufferings. But that's a lie: in fact we want an end to our sufferings.

One morning Vadim came into the kitchen, and without looking at anyone said: 'Mother's dead.'

The door was unlocked and we all went in. Anfisa Maximovna was lying flat and heavy on the bed; she didn't seem to be at rest, she looked as though she'd been struggling on her death bed. Her face was a greenish colour, stern and condemning.

'Thank God her sufferings are over,' said Kapa. 'God rest the soul of Thy newly departed slave. . . '

'We all go in the end!' barked Panka. Ada wept in a crackling, hen-like voice.

Kapa washed and tidied her and we laid out the body on the table. 'She's all skin and bone, but she's very heavy,' said Kapa. 'A dead body's always heavy. That's because it contains a living soul.'

There was nothing Kapa didn't know about death and funerals. 'She's not the first I've buried, thank God! I wash them and I bind them and I lay them in the coffin. You have to cover up all the mirrors, otherwise the soul will see itself and it's bad for the soul to see itself in the mirror. You have to sew covers for them, that way you'll be sewing eternal life for the soul.'

On the dead woman's forehead Kapa put a strip of paper with a prayer – Anfisa was a Christian person after all, she said, even though she was an unbeliever. Vadim came into the room. 'Take that off!' he said.

He decided to bury her at the crematorium. Kapa protested and spoke of the Day of Judgement: when the Angel blew his trumpet and everyone rose up from the grave and was united with their body, those who were cremated would have no bodies to return to. He payed no attention to this. But, in general, during those days before the funeral he was gentle and polite to everyone – he even brought me a chair to sit on. He kept tossing back his head as though trying to drive away importunate thoughts.

[39]

Anfisa Maximovna was to be buried on the day before the October holiday. There was a lot to do at the House of the Child that day as we were preparing a concert for the following morning and everyone was hurriedly sewing costumes, ironing and making a lot of noise. Then my first soloist, Vasilii Sishkin, suddenly lost his voice and developed a cough, and we had to replace him at short notice with someone else who didn't want to do it and cried. Then we learnt that there would be a commission coming to visit us next day, and the directress became extremely nervous and made us all repeat our cantata ten times, and as always happens when things are rushed, it didn't go at all well. The piano sounded horrible and one key was jammed, but the tuner had already started on the next day's celebrations and was very much the worse for drink. In short, it was bedlam.

The cremation was fixed for seven o'clock. I'd decided to go to the crematorium straight from work, but the rehearsal had gone so badly that I feared I wouldn't make it in time. Just after five I told the directress that I had to leave; she waved me away with a vinegary face, observing that there was still plenty of time and that one shouldn't put oneself above the common good. I said nothing. There was only just enough time, in fact – the first bus ride would take over an hour, and then I'd have to change. And a taxi was out of the question on a day like this . . . I went out onto the street. The frozen ground rang under foot, the air was dry and cold, a full moon sailed overhead, swooping and plunging into the mad bright clouds, then leaping out again, its light flooding the street. Then suddenly I saw a green light shining not too far away. Miracle of miracles, a taxi! I raised my arm and the car rolled up, skidding over the frozen ruts.

'To the crematorium!' I said, and we rolled off.

'Burying someone, are you?' asked the driver. I nodded.

'Relative?'

'No, a friend.'

'Well that's not so bad then.'

We drove through Moscow, festive and lively, festooned with coloured lamps, the facades of the buildings covered in brightly lit portraits. Red calico flapped in the wind, and the city, seized up in the general excitement, assumed a dignified air and took flight. Crowds of people headed for the shops, music poured from the loudspeakers and here and there staggered those who had started celebrating early. The car tore through the bustling, brightly lit city. I tried not to look at the meter clicking ominously away – I didn't know if I'd have enough money. Eventually we arrived, and fortunately I did have enough money, even with some to spare. 'All the best with your funeral!' said the driver, accepting a tip.

I went into the hall, his parting works ringing in my ears. It turned out that I was an hour early. It was just six.

* *

The hall was filled with the strange, damp, bitter smell of autumn flowers, in people's hands and in coffins – feathery crysanthemums and delicate asters resembling little pink, convulsively clutched fists. I hadn't brought any flowers, I hadn't had time. I hadn't done anything . . .

I looked around with a certain morbid curiosity at everything that was going on there, observing it all despite my sadness – or perhaps because of it . . . I had a long time to wait, and several funerals took place in this time. They were all so depressingly similiar. The next coffin (they all had identical yellow old men lying in them) was brought in and laid on a side pedestal while the mourners wept and talked quietly amongst themselves. Then the administrator, an elderly woman in a bright green cardigan, with painted lips and a little hammer in her hand, said: 'Bring the coffin over!' They lit the central chandelier above the main pedestal, and the men carrried the coffin into the centre, clutching their caps under their arms or handing them to the women. Jostling diffidently, they placed the coffin on some boards covered in black velvet, then grew confused. 'The head facing forward please!' shouted the administrator. They leaned the coffin lid against the wall (it fell twice), then everyone clustered behind the balustrade surrounding the coffin and the organist started playing. He was accompanied by a solo violinist with a bored expression, and they'd play either Chopin's *Funeral March* or Massenet's *Elegy*. It never varied. The women would cry and some would wail, yet it was all extremely quiet and decorous. The administrator in the green cardigan would say: 'Relatives, say farewell!' Another outburst of weeping. People went right up to the coffin, kneeling or bowing before it, putting their lips to the dead one's forehead and wailing quietly. Then the administrator would announce 'Last farewell!', the coffin was nailed down (with a few dry little taps, traditionally symbolising the end), the music started up again and the coffin on its pedestal was lowered. Above it fluttered the folds of black velvet, with a little flower from someone else's funeral trembling on top. The chandelier was immediately extinguished and the relatives, supporting some female figure (probably the old man's wife or daughter) would leave the central room and go out of the hall. In less than three minutes the next funeral would start. Once again it was the same 'bring the coffin over!', the same cluster of men, the same placing of the coffin, the same music, the hammering, the lowering of the coffin, the trembling flower on the velvet folds . . . It was terrible, but not with the usual terror of death, it was the deadly uniformity, the routine nature of the whole procedure which was terrible.

There was one strange detail that struck me though. The same man kept appearing amongst the mourners. He was dark, fairly young and rather handsome, and he would go up to each coffin, mingle with the group of mourners, stare intently into the face of the old man, then carry the coffin with the others, stopping by the balustrade and weeping when the music played. Who he was and why he wept over every coffin was a mystery to me. Maybe he was mad, maybe an actor learning to cry, maybe someone who had buried someone very dear to him here . . .

The last family was already saying farewell, and my heart sank painfully. Then the next coffin was brought in, and this was ours, mine. And all at once the institutional walls of that hall shone with my own grief as I saw Anfisa's face in the coffin – how the last eleven hours had changed her! Her head lay on a pillow edged with some coarse lace, probably made of paper. Someone else had laid her in her coffin and combed her hair. She was surrounded by a few modest and meagre flowers and the people standing round her were equally modest and meagre. Vadim, looking very pale and handsome, was in front, his feet planted wide apart, and behind him were the inhabitants of the flat – our communal family. Then the teachers from the nursery-school and the janitor from our yard, tragically twisting his cap in his hands. The coffin was carried by Vadim, the janitor and the driver of the hearse. There were few men there, and the coffin swayed precariously. Ada Efimovna jumped up and grasped it with her slender hand. 'You don't have to!' said Vadim with twisted lips.

Then they stopped with the coffin. Yet again the organ played Massenet's *Elegy*, but this time the music overwhelmed me. My eyes stung and I felt the tears streaming down my cheeks. The sensation, forgotten for all these years, was one of heart-rending happiness. I welcomed the tears with delight and I wept, freely, publicly and profusely, thanking Anfisa for having lived. The organ stopped playing and I stopped crying. 'Relatives, say farewell!'

My dear one. I kissed Anfisa's marble brow. I didn't see Vadim's face at the last moment, only his angry, hunched shoulders. I involuntarily put out my hand and touched him. He turned round with the expression of a whipped dog and brushed my hand off his shoulder with his cheek – as though he were kissing me. The music started up again, the coffin was lowered, the black velvet folds closed, the same little flower trembled, the chandeliers were extinguished. We began to disperse. They were already bringing on another coffin.

* *

After the funeral Vadim returned home. Everything was so clean and tidy, the bed had been removed and the room seemed large and echoing. His life was empty. 'Kara-ti-ti-kara!' he said and laughed, then clutched his head and groaned.

Later, at the funeral feast, he drank a lot and didn't speak much. Kapa presided. No one wept.

When he woke up next morning it took him a while to recollect what had happened. An oblique shaft of sunlight sidled across the wall, over the green squares and triangles of the wallpaper. The squares and triangles were brighter where the bed had stood. Elsewhere they'd faded . . .

That night Vadim had a dream. And in this dream he saw in a flash all the sins he had committed against his mother. There were many of them, so many that he broke down and wept. When he woke up his pillow was wet.

That bitter, tear-soaked pillow spelt the start of a new life for him.

[41]

At night it snows or rains as before, and the ship of widows sails on.